HENRY
and the
Guardians
of the Lost

Books by Jenny Nimmo

Midnight for Charlie Bone
Charlie Bone and the Time Twister
Charlie Bone and the Blue Boa
Charlie Bone and the Castle of Mirrors
Charlie Bone and the Hidden King
Charlie Bone and the Wilderness Wolf
Charlie Bone and the Shadow of Badlock
Charlie Bone and the Red Knight

Henry and the Guardians of the Lost

The Secret Kingdom
The Secret Kingdom: The Stones of Ravenglass
The Secret Kingdom: Leopard's Gold

The Snow Spider (Modern Classics edition)
The Snow Spider Trilogy

Henry

and the Guardians of the Lost

JENNY NIMMO

EGMONT

EGMONT

We bring stories to life

First published in paperback in Great Britain 2016
by Egmont UK Limited
The Yellow Building, 1 Nicholas Road, London W11 4AN

Text copyright © 2016 Jenny Nimmo
Cover illustration by George Ermos

The moral rights of the author and illustrator have been asserted

ISBN 978 1 4052 8087 7

www.egmont.co.uk

63325/1

A CIP catalogue record for this title is available from the British Library

Printed and bound by CPI Group (UK) Ltd, Croydon, CR0 4YY

Stay safe online. Any website addresses listed in this book are correct
at the time of going to print. However, Egmont is not responsible for content
hosted by third parties. Please be aware that online content can be subject
to change and websites can contain content that is unsuitable for children.
We advise that all children are supervised when using the internet.

For Max, with love.

CONTENTS

CHAPTER ONE
The Yellow Letter

The yellow letter arrived on a Saturday, otherwise Henry would have been at school. The envelope was such a bright, sunny colour, no one would have believed that it contained a bombshell

There had been a storm in the night and the postman was late. Henry went out to see if the wild ocean had flooded the road. He knew he shouldn't stand so close to the edge of the cliff, but he had survived so many dark and dangerous events, he had decided that nothing could finish him off. That was before he knew the contents of the yellow envelope.

Henry lived with his aunt, Pearl, and a black and white cat called Enkidu. Pearl wasn't his real aunt, she was more of a minder, but she was distantly related to Henry, and also his cousin, Charlie. Henry's parents had died long ago, nearly a hundred years in his father's case. How could that be, you might ask, if Henry was only twelve?

1

That was his secret.

Henry's life had changed in an instant, almost a century ago. He had been alone in the great hall of his uncle's gloomy house when a large and beautiful marble had come rolling towards him. Unaware of the danger, Henry had picked it up and looked into it. He had been thrust into the future, and had lived in the present for almost two years, but in all that time he hadn't grown. Not one inch.

Henry's home was a small white-washed house perched halfway up a rugged cliff. For obvious reasons the house was called Ocean View. It was a place of safety for a boy whose past was almost too incredible to be believed.

Frank, the postman, arrived at last. He was a wiry, cheerful person with a wide smile and large, pink ears. He never complained about the steep lane that led up to the house nor the road below that was frequently puddled with sea water.

Henry met Frank at the front door. 'Hullo, Frank. Have you had a bad time?' Henry looked up at the rain-filled clouds.

'Not so bad.' Frank placed a bundle of mail in Henry's hands.

The yellow letter was on top.

'Interesting!' Frank tapped the stamp in the corner. 'Diplodocus, is it?'

'Iguanodon,' said Henry.

'I'll learn them one day.' Frank grinned and got back into his van. 'Give my regards to Auntie Pearl!' he called as he sped off.

Henry regarded the yellow envelope. The name and address had been written in a large sloping hand. There was no mistaking Aunt Treasure's round dots and sweeping tails. He took the mail into the kitchen where his aunt was making a chocolate cake.

Pearl was a small, round woman with dark, greying hair and permanently rosy cheeks. Henry placed the letters as close to the mixing bowl as he dared. He waited, hopefully, for Pearl to pick up the yellow envelope. She glanced at it and smiled. 'Ah, from my sister.'

But the letter wasn't opened until the chocolate cake was in the oven and Pearl's hands were clean. Henry tried not to appear nosey, but he was keen to know what Treasure had to say. He sensed a secret, something too important to be said on the phone.

Pearl took ages to read the letter. The more she read, the more she frowned. It seemed that she couldn't quite comprehend what her sister had written. And then she opened her eyes, very wide, and dropped the letter. Clasping her face in both hands, she said breathily, 'Henry, go and pack your bag.'

'What?' Henry couldn't believe Pearl's instruction.

'Now!' she commanded. 'Now, Henry. Not a moment to lose.'

'But . . .'

'Didn't you hear what I said?' Agitation made her words sound like a kind of scream.

'You said pack a bag. But why?'

'I'll explain later.' Pearl tore off her apron and ran to the kitchen door. 'Come on, Henry. This is no time to dream.'

'I'm not dreaming,' Henry mumbled as he followed Pearl upstairs. 'Or maybe I am, because I'm not sure that this is really happening. Charlie was coming today.'

'Not now,' said Pearl.

'But we'd made plans. I've been thinking about them all week. Charlie is the only –'

'You can see your cousin when . . .' Pearl hesitated. 'When all this is over.'

'All what? Charlie's my best friend, and I only see him at weekends.'

Pearl ignored him. 'Pack everything you might need: pyjamas, wash-bag, clean underwear . . .' She reeled off a list. Henry wondered how he was going to fit it all in.

Enkidu, Henry's cat, was asleep on his bed.

'We're going away,' Henry told his large, exceptionally fluffy friend. 'So who's going to look after you?'

Enkidu didn't appear to be concerned. He was snoring.

Henry began to throw things into his bag, while Pearl shouted from her room. 'Hurry, hurry, hurry!' And then she called, 'Henry, take something you love.'

Henry looked at Enkidu. 'OK,' he called back.

Throwing stuff out of his bag, he picked up Enkidu and put him in the bag. Enkidu didn't mind. He didn't even wake up. But he stopped snoring. If he hadn't, things might have turned out very differently.

Henry zipped up the bag, leaving a tiny gap at the end to give the cat some air.

Pearl was already thumping down the stairs. Henry ran after her. He grabbed his anorak from the hallstand as Pearl opened the front door. 'Come on, come on!' she said.

'Can't you tell me where we're going?' Henry complained.

'Somewhere safe,' Pearl murmured. 'It's complicated.'

But I was safe here, wasn't I? Henry thought.

Just in time, Pearl remembered to turn off the oven. She didn't bother to remove the cake. When they were both outside Pearl locked the front door. Henry saw that her hands were shaking. A bad sign; Henry thought Pearl was a risky driver at the best of times. He waited while she backed the car out of the lean-to beside the house.

'Hop in!' called Pearl when she had manoeuvred on to the lane.

Henry put his bag carefully on to the back seat, then jumped in beside his aunt. He noticed that Pearl had only brought a handbag. There was no sign of anything for her overnight things.

'Aren't you –?' Henry began.

'Hold tight,' said Pearl.

They swooped down the muddy lane and bounced on to the wet road. After ten minutes they turned off on to a narrow track. Henry had never gone this way before. Half an hour later they emerged on to a busy main road. On and on they went, through villages and small towns, over bleak brown moors and narrow bridges, through tunnels and around forests. The light began to fade and evening mists drifted up from the damp fields.

'You said you would tell me why we're doing this.' Henry's head felt heavy and he could hardly keep his eyes open.

Pearl took a breath. 'People were coming.' Her voice became deep and grave. 'Someone talked about you, Henry. We don't know who, it could have been quite accidental. But anyway, these . . . these beasts got wind of you, who you are and how you haven't grown.

And they would have taken you, Henry, for . . .' her hands tensed on the wheel, 'who knows what. But certainly I couldn't have stopped them.'

Henry shivered. He was suddenly wide awake. 'The yellow letter,' he said. 'It was a warning.'

'Yes, from Treasure. She tried to ring but our phone was out of order, and we don't get a mobile signal in our faraway part of the world.'

'But why, Auntie Pearl? Why were they so determined to take me?'

She took a moment to reply, and then she said quietly, 'They believe that you, and others like you, hold the key to obtaining the greatest prize on earth.'

'And what's that?' asked Henry, somehow dreading the answer.

'I think you can guess,' his aunt said gravely. 'The secret of eternal youth.'

'Because I haven't grown,' Henry whispered.

They drove in silence for a while, and his mind raced so fast he began to feel dizzy. A loud noise from his stomach distracted him. He thought of the chocolate cake left in the oven. 'Did you bring sandwiches?' he asked, without much hope. 'Or biscuits?'

Pearl shook her head. 'I'm sorry, Henry.'

Henry tried not to think about food, but he couldn't help thinking of the chocolate cake, with loads of chocolate icing on the top. He could even taste it.

They drove through a dark, dense pine forest, emerging, at last, on to a wide road where lights twinkled in the distance.

'There'll be somewhere to eat,' Pearl said cheerfully.

And there was. Halfway down the high street of a friendly-looking village they found a small, bright cafe with steamy windows and red checked tablecloths.

Henry tried to forget the people that were coming to get him, while he concentrated on his food. He had almost finished his large plate of sausages, chips and beans when he suddenly remembered his cat.

'Enkidu!' he cried, dropping his fork.

'He'll be fine,' said Pearl, in a matter-of-fact voice.

'He's in the car,' said Henry, 'in my bag.'

'What?' Pearl scrunched up her eyes. 'How could you be so stupid?'

'You told me to bring something I loved,' said Henry defiantly.

Pearl gave a loud sigh of exasperation. She put her keys on the table. 'You'd better let him out. He'll want to go for a pee.'

It sounded as if Pearl hoped Enkidu would go off and not return. Henry grabbed his remaining sausage and dashed outside. Enkidu ate the sausage gratefully, had a pee in a muddy verge, covered it with leaves and happily jumped back into the car.

Henry was about to run back into the cafe when

Pearl came out of the door. 'In the car, Henry,' she said. 'We must keep going.'

Henry hadn't finished all his chips, but Pearl looked so stern, he didn't like to mention it.

They drove through the darkness, their headlights shining on long, winter grass and high, wild hedges. On and on.

'How d'you know where to go, Auntie Pearl?' Henry's voice sounded small and fearful.

'A map in my head,' she said. 'My sister put it there.' And there was the ghost of a smile in her voice. 'We're looking for an arch with carvings on it, birds and beasts and flowers and things.'

Henry became aware of a wall beside them. Not the usual kind of wall, but a screen of trees, laced with stone. A wall that vanished now and then, like a memory, a dream, a wall that could never be touched, a wall that would never let you through. And, all at once, there was the arch that would allow them into a place that had appeared to be forbidden.

'Not birds and beasts,' Henry whispered. For the carvings in the pale stone pillars of the arch were not birds, they were the bones of sad, fragile creatures that perhaps no longer existed.

'It's nearly midnight,' said Pearl. 'We're just in time.'

'Midnight already?' Henry sat up very straight

in his seat. Pearl accelerated a little, as though she wanted to get through the arch as soon as possible. They passed under the big, ghostly stones and emerged into total darkness.

The engine stopped. The headlights went out. Perhaps they were not in the car at all, for Henry couldn't feel the rim of his seat, or his safety belt. He could hardly breathe. The darkness all about them was so dense and so black it seemed to smother them.

Enkidu growled.

CHAPTER TWO
Timeless

Henry reached for Pearl's hand. He could feel nothing.

'It'll be all right, Henry.' Her voice came from a long way away.

Slowly the impenetrable darkness began to lighten. The smothering feeling lifted and Henry could hear the reassuring purr of the engine. They were moving again, and as they moved a peculiar thing happened. Ahead of them the sun began to rise; higher and higher, faster and faster. The night clouds melted away, leaving the sky a clear ice-blue.

'There,' said Pearl, pulling down her sunshield. 'All is well.'

'Is it?' Henry was baffled by the sudden appearance of the sun. What had happened to the hours between midnight and sunrise? 'You said there were birds on the arch. Those weren't birds.'

'Treasure's writing is a little . . . untidy.' Pearl gave an unconvincing chuckle.

They were travelling along a road that ran between rows of warehouses. Beyond them a vast forest stretched as far as the eye could see. The huge doors in every warehouse had been thrown wide open, as though in expectation of some giant delivery.

'Weird,' said Henry. 'We seem so far from anywhere.'

'The equinox,' his aunt murmured.

'The equinox?' Henry inquired.

'The sun tips over the horizon,' she said, 'and night is as long as day.' It was the only explanation that she seemed prepared to give.

When they had passed the warehouses, a church spire came into view, and then a cluster of roofs. Pearl was driving dangerously fast, Henry thought. Perhaps she was trying to catch a mirage before it disappeared. But as they drew closer to the buildings, Henry could see that it *was* a mirage; they were about to enter a small town.

'Timeless' said a sign beside the road.

Henry could see nothing special about the place, except that the frost and sunlight made it look very bright.

'There it is,' cried Pearl. 'I'm dying for a cup of tea.'

They stopped outside a cafe with a pink and orange awning. Above the awning, the words, 'Martha's Cafe' had been painted in blue and orange, the top of each letter decorated with a pink cupcake. Behind the cafe, trees loomed – their naked branches festooned with ivy.

Henry was hungry again. Pearl ordered eggs on toast for them both, tea for herself and hot chocolate for Henry. Her mood had changed again. Her smile had gone. She ate quickly and when she had finished her breakfast, she stood up, saying, 'I'm just going to tidy my hair.' And then she came round the table and kissed Henry's cheek.

It was the first time that Pearl had kissed him before going to the toilet. He hoped she wasn't going to make a habit of it.

Henry finished his meal and drained his cup. Pearl was taking a long time. Her hair had looked perfectly tidy. After all she'd been inside a car all day, or was it all night? He noticed two children sitting at a table by the window: a boy and a girl, about his age. They wore purple-coloured sweaters and grey trousers. The girl had long brown hair, a small nose and a wide, serious face. They boy looked exactly the same, only his hair was short. They were both staring at him.

Henry returned their stare and then, feeling self-conscious looked down at his plate. Several minutes passed. What was Pearl doing? He didn't like to go and look in the Ladies' cloakroom.

The children were still staring at him. Henry felt

uncomfortable. All at once the girl stood up and came over to his table.

'Are you meeting someone here?' she asked.

'Er, no,' said Henry.

'Was that your gran who just went to the cloakroom?'

'My aunt,' said Henry.

'Well . . .' The girl swung from foot to foot. 'I think she's forgotten you.'

'No, she hasn't,' said Henry indignantly. 'She's just taking a long time.'

The girl shook her head regretfully. 'We just saw her get into a blue car that was parked outside.'

'I expect she was fetching something she'd forgotten,' said Henry, wondering why Pearl had gone out without telling him. He had his back to the entrance and couldn't see the cloakroom door.

'She drove away,' said the girl.

Henry felt a bit sick. He chewed his lip. 'She couldn't have.'

The girl pulled out a chair and sat opposite him, then the boy came over and stood between them. He had a calm, confident expression. 'She hasn't come back,' he said. 'I've been watching.'

Henry was slightly annoyed. What business did these children have, watching him and his aunt? He felt his heart thumping and told himself he wasn't worried.

'D'you want to come home with us?' asked the girl.

'No,' Henry said fiercely. 'I'll wait here. I know my aunt will come back.'

'We'll wait with you.' The boy pulled a chair across from another table and sat down.

Henry could see now that the boy was older than the girl; he was also quite a bit taller. He obviously liked to take control of certain situations.

'My name's Peter,' said the boy. 'Peter Reed. And this is Penny.' He nodded at the girl who gave Henry a weak smile.

Henry thought it would be churlish not to give them a bit more information about himself, so he told them his name and where he had come from. When he described the hurried drive through the night, Peter gave Penny a slightly furtive smile. Henry kept his secret to himself. In the friendly school at home, they were used to him and never pried. But now he was in unfamiliar territory and he knew he must be 'on his guard'.

'We always come here early on Sunday mornings,' said Peter. 'You get the best doughnuts.'

'Want one?' asked Penny.

Henry hesitated. *Nothing wrong with a doughnut,* he thought. 'OK,' he said. 'Thanks.'

Peter went to the counter to buy three doughnuts. When he came back, Henry glanced at the clock on the wall. It had said half-past twelve when he and

Pearl had come in. It still did. He looked at his watch: half-past twelve.

'The clock's stopped,' Henry remarked. 'So has my watch.'

'No time here,' said Penny. 'Not in Timeless.'

'No time like the present,' Peter said with a grin.

'Time flies,' trilled Penny. 'Time stands still.'

Henry had an urge to tell them both to shut up. He felt angry and confused.

'You'd better come home with us,' said Peter. 'Our parents will help you.'

Henry didn't like being bossed. 'I think I should stay and wait for my aunt,' he said, biting in to his doughnut.

'Leave a note for your aunt with Martha,' Penny suggested. 'Tell her you've gone to Number Five, Ruby Drive. You can't stay here all day.'

Henry could see that she had a point. The cafe was filling up and people were searching for spare tables. When the doughnuts were eaten, he went to the counter and left a note with the friendly woman called Martha. The note said:

Dear Auntie Pearl,
    You didn't come back, so I've gone to Number Five, Ruby Drive. I'll wait for you there.
    Love from Henry

When they stepped outside a large black and white cat came running up to them.

'Enkidu!' Henry knelt and flung his arms around the cat, burying his face in the long, soft fur. 'Did Pearl throw you out?'

'He was already out when the car left,' said Peter. 'I noticed him sitting behind the bins.'

'Hiding,' said Penny. 'He wanted to stay.'

Henry gathered Enkidu into his arms. 'Thank you! Thank you, Enkidu,' he whispered in the cat's hairy ear.

Number Five, Ruby Drive was only a few minutes away. It was a red brick, modern-looking house with a small front garden and a path paved with red and black tiles.

Peter unlocked the front door and Penny followed him into the house. Henry hesitated on the doorstep.

'Come on,' said the Reeds.

Henry carried Enkidu into Number Five. It seemed welcoming. There were red tiles on the floor and the wall was covered with framed photos of Peter and Penny holding silver cups, bronze medals and official-looking certificates. Henry had never won anything.

Peter and Penny led Henry past a red-carpeted staircase to a room at the back of the house.

'Look, Mum,' said Peter, opening the door with a bit of a flourish, 'another one. Ta da!' He shoved Henry into a room that seemed to be crammed with children; three small ones to be precise.

Two toddlers and a baby were playing on the floor. A woman with short brown hair and spectacles stood at the kitchen sink, peeling potatoes. She turned to Henry and said, 'Ah! I see. What's your name, dear?' Her eyebrows were raised in an interested but not exactly friendly way.

Henry didn't reply. He was wondering what they meant by 'another one'.

'His name is Henry Yewbeam,' Peter told his mother.

'Come in, dear, and have a cup of something,' said Mrs Reed.

'Tea,' said Penny firmly. She filled a kettle and put it on the gas stove.

Peter pulled out a chair, saying, 'Sit down, Henry. You'll be OK. We'll try to make sure of that.'

Try? thought Henry. He sat down and put Enkidu on his lap.

'That's a very fine animal,' Mrs Reed remarked.

'His name's Enkidu,' said Henry. 'I hope you don't mind cats.'

'Not at all.' Mrs Reed smiled. 'Our old tabby died a month ago, and we've been looking for a replacement. Your cat can use Tibby's cat-flap.'

Henry's grip on Enkidu tightened. 'What did you mean when you said you'd found another one?' he asked Peter.

Penny put a cup of tea in front of Henry. 'There was a girl,' she explained. 'Just like you, left in Martha's cafe, all alone, no mum or dad, just a suitcase. Mum brought her home, didn't you, Mum?'

Henry stared at Mrs Reed. 'What happened to her?'

'She disappeared,' said Mrs Reed in a matter-of-fact way.

'Disappeared?' Henry's voice was tight and dry. 'Did you phone the police?'

There was a troubling silence while Mrs Reed took off her apron and sat at the table. 'There are no police here, dear,' she said, patting Henry's hand.

'No police,' Henry croaked. 'None at all? Not even one?'

'We have the mayor and his councillors,' Mrs Reed told him in a firm voice. 'They uphold the law. And then there are the henchmen, of course. Even they couldn't find the girl.'

'Oh.' Henry felt weighed down by all this unwelcome news. The faces round the table were friendly enough, and the noise of chortling toddlers and boiling potatoes, and the sunshine outside the window should have made him feel cheerful, but he couldn't rid himself of the thought that if someone else had been left in Martha's Cafe, and then disappeared, he might disappear too.

Mrs Reed suggested that the children should go into the garden until lunchtime. Henry refused. So Peter took him up to his bedroom. Enkidu followed. He was keen on bedrooms.

There was a spare bed in Peter's room, already made up for his friend, Bill, who often slept over. 'So we're always prepared, you see,' said Peter.

Enkidu jumped on the bed, curled up and closed his eyes.

Lunch wasn't tasty but it was very filling. In the afternoon Peter and Penny persuaded Henry to walk between them a little way up the road. Timeless looked like any other small town. A few of the neighbours waved, and a friend cycling past cried, 'Hi, Peter!'

Henry noticed that there were very few cars, and several people were pale and dishevelled. Peter saw Henry staring at a woman whose face was so white she looked like a ghost. She appeared to be exhausted and could barely put one foot in front of the other.

'She tried to get through,' Peter said with a grin.

'Through?' said Henry. 'Through what?'

'You'll find out.' Penny gave a giggle. 'You'd think they'd know better by now.'

Henry felt very uneasy. He wanted to ask more, but guessed that no one would tell him anything – yet. He'd have to find out for himself.

At the end of the road a sharp rise led to a grand

house standing behind ornate iron railings. It was four storeys high, with a steep slate roof and many sparkling windows. Shiny brass studs decorated the tall front door, and there were two door knockers. One a plain ring, the other a large hand.

'The mayor's house,' Polly told Henry.

As she spoke the door opened and two men walked out. They wore midnight-blue suits, the jackets covered in gleaming insignia and the breeches tucked into tall polished boots. Each man carried an iron club and wore a steel helmet.

'Henchmen,' Peter said, almost reverently. 'They keep the law very efficiently.'

I bet they do, thought Henry, observing the long, thick clubs.

The children turned and walked back to Number Five. A cold wind had sprung up and Henry put his hands into his pockets to keep them warm. His fingers curled around a scrap of paper.

At first he thought it was an old note from school that he'd forgotten to give Pearl. But when he opened the folded paper he saw that the note was *from* Pearl. She had obviously been in a hurry; the writing was slanting and spidery. It said:

Forgive me, Henry. I did it for the best. I've no time to explain. I have to be out within the hour.

Go round to the trees behind the cafe. Keep yourself hidden and wait for Mr Lazlo. Ask him where the white bird flies. He must reply, 'In the Little House.' Anything else and he's the wrong person. Tell no one!

I'll think of you every day.

Your loving aunt,

Pearl x

Henry pushed the note back into his pocket and kept on walking. Polly and Peter paid no attention. They probably thought he'd found an old message from a friend.

They reached the gate at Number Five and, all at once, Henry felt uncomfortably shaky. He stood by the gate while the others walked up to the front door. *I'm in the wrong place,* he thought. *Tell no one,* the note said. So how could he explain it if he decided to return to the hiding place behind the cafe?

'You OK, Henry?' Peter asked.

Henry nodded. He smiled uncertainly.

'Maybe it's jet lag?' Penny offered.

'I didn't fly here,' Henry mumbled. Pearl wasn't coming back and he'd missed the person he was supposed to meet. He followed the Reeds into the house. Where else could he go?

Mr Reed appeared at suppertime. He had a wide

face and thinning black hair. His cheeks were rosy and he smiled easily. He shook Henry's hand and patted his shoulder, saying, 'Things will be all right, Henry. We'll make sure of that.'

How? Henry wondered.

'Should we let the mayor know?' Mrs Reed asked her husband.

Mr Reed shook his head. 'Not yet.' He darted a look at Henry and smiled. 'We haven't heard Henry's story.'

Henry had nothing more to tell. He certainly wasn't going to reveal his secret to these strangers, or mention Pearl's note.

They sat round the kitchen table, eating bacon, beans and eggs. Enkidu was given some bacon fat. The smallest baby was in bed, the toddlers ate noisily. No one else said much. Henry kept thinking of the note in his anorak pocket.

'So are you going to tell us why your aunt brought you here?' Mr Reed asked Henry halfway through the meal.

Henry hesitated. He had to say something, and he wouldn't be giving anything away by describing his journey. 'She got a letter, my aunt. I don't know what it said. She never told me. She was in an awful hurry. We drove all day and then went through an arch carved with bones and stuff. The next moment we were in total darkness, and the car was floating, then suddenly it was morning.' He took a deep breath. 'We went to Martha's Cafe, and when I wasn't looking my aunt left.'

Mr Reed nodded. He didn't seem at all surprised. 'And your aunt gave you no instructions, nothing to indicate where you should go, what you were to do?'

Henry thought of the note. *Tell no one.* He shook his head.

Peter gave him an odd look. It made Henry feel uncomfortable. He couldn't stop his cheeks from reddening. He wondered if the Reeds noticed. He felt very hot.

'Just like the other one,' Penny said thoughtfully. 'She disappeared in the night, after curfew.'

'Curfew?' Henry said. 'Curfews are for prisons and . . . and wars, not normal towns.'

The Reeds all laughed. What was so funny? No one explained.

After supper, Mr and Mrs Reed took the toddlers upstairs for their bath. Penny did her homework at one end of the kitchen table, while Henry taught Peter how to play Battleships at the other end. The room was lit by gas lamps that popped and fizzed from the wall. Henry found that he could hardly keep his eyes open and remembered that he and Pearl had driven through the night. A large old clock hung above the stove. It was stained and rusty and, like the clock in

Martha's Cafe, it had stopped at half past twelve. He asked Peter if he knew the time.

'We won't know for sure until the town crier comes round,' Peter replied casually.

'Don't any of your clocks work? Don't you have a watch?' Henry asked anxiously.

'Mm, no,' said Peter, concentrating on his next move.

Henry felt a bit light-headed. 'I think I'd like to go to bed,' he said.

'Good idea.' Peter put down his pencil. 'I want to finish my book before curfew.'

That word again. Henry asked, 'What happens at curfew?'

'Of course, you don't have curfew, do you?' Peter said in a patronising voice.

'I have bedtime,' said Henry. 'At least I used to.'

'Ah, well, the town crier comes round ringing his bell and telling us it's ten o'clock. Everyone has to be indoors, and all the lamps and candles out.' Peter said this as if it was the most normal thing in the world.

'Even the street lights?'

'The gas lights? Of course. And then the henchmen come round with a lantern, checking for curfew breakers.'

'And if anyone breaks the curfew? What then?'

'Don't ask,' said Peter. An unsatisfactory answer.

They were given candles in brass saucers to take to bed.

'I expect you have e-l-e-c-t-r-i-c-i-t-y at home,' said Peter, enunciating jokingly.

Puzzled, Henry said, 'Most people do.'

Peter chuckled. 'Not us. We do have a telephone, though. Just us and a few others. The mayor has a generator.'

Henry was glad to see that Enkidu hadn't moved from the bed. The big cat was obviously making up for his undignified journey. When Henry got into bed he pushed his feet under Enkidu's heavy body. It was comforting to feel his friend so close.

'Don't think I'll read tonight,' said Peter, blowing out his candle.

Henry did the same, but he lay awake, staring into the dark. Was he safe in this house? And if he got back to the cafe, would Mr Lazlo be there? He doubted it. He was drifting off to sleep when he heard a bell ringing outside the house. A voice called, 'Ten o'clock and all's well.' Soon after this, the rhythmic sound of marching boots grew louder and louder. Tired as he was, curiosity drove Henry to the window. He looked down on a column of men, their helmets glinting in the fitful light of the moon. Henchmen.

Later, much later, Henry's eyes opened again. There wasn't a sound anywhere. But he was suddenly wide awake. He went to the window.

The moon was higher and brighter now. Peering through a gap in the curtains, Henry looked down at the road. A black horse stood by the garden gate. Its rider, a cloaked figure in a large beret, was looking up at Henry's window. The man had a thick black beard and one gloved hand covered his mouth, as though he were puzzled or uncertain. In spite of the man's forbidding appearance, Henry had to restrain a sudden urge to call out to him.

The man turned his head and looked up the road. The next minute he and the horse were gone. If it hadn't been for the fading clatter of hooves, Henry might have believed that horse and rider had never existed.

And then came another sound. The heavy tread of approaching henchmen.

CHAPTER THREE
Henchmen

Henry slept deeply. When he woke up Peter had gone. Henry crept downstairs, wondering what time it was. The sun was high. Perhaps it was lunchtime. There was no sign of Enkidu.

The kitchen was deserted but breakfast hadn't been cleared away. The table was strewn with boxes of cereal, jams, butter and a rack of toast.

Mrs Reed popped her head round the door and said, 'Help yourself, Henry. Peter and Penny have gone to school.'

'Have you seen my cat?' asked Henry.

'Not a whisker,' said Mrs Reed. It was difficult to tell if she was joking.

After a large bowl of cereal and several pieces of toast, Henry was just wondering what to drink when Mrs Reed looked in again and asked, 'How old are you, Henry? The headmaster will want to know.'

Henry reached for the orange juice. 'Why?' he said.

'Am I going to school?'

'Just a thought.' Mrs Reed gave him her cool smile. 'We have to find something for you to do, don't we, until . . .?' She seemed unable to finish her sentence.

Until what? Henry wondered. *How long am I going to be here?*

'Nine?' asked Mrs Reed impatiently. 'Ten? Have you forgotten how old you are?'

Henry couldn't see the point of lying. His brain was older than a ten-year-old's. She would think he was small for his age. Nothing more. 'Twelve,' he said quickly.

'Ah.' Mrs Reed retreated.

After breakfast Henry wandered into the hall. What was he to do with himself? The Reeds didn't appear to own a television set or a radio, or even an electronic game. He was about to mount the stairs when Mrs Reed came out of a bedroom. 'I'm sure you'll find a book to read,' she said. 'I'll ring the headmaster in a minute. Don't leave the house, will you?'

'I want to look for my cat,' said Henry.

'Don't leave the house,' Mrs Reed said harshly. 'The cat will come back.'

Henry went into the sitting room. The shelves were full of rather dull-looking books. Henry pulled out a heavy volume entitled, *Sailing Ships of the World*. Some of the ships popped up when the book was laid flat on the table. He was admiring a sixteenth-century galleon when Mrs Reed made her phone call from the hall. There was something quiet and sly in her tone. Henry could only make out the occasional word. He assumed she felt awkward explaining his small size, and didn't want him to overhear.

The phone call ended and Mrs Reed went back upstairs to where the baby was screaming.

For several minutes Henry continued to admire the Tudor galleon, observing the construction of the sails and the multitude of ropes and knots. A sudden tap on the window made him look round. Enkidu was outside, staring in at him from the sill.

Henry jumped up. 'Enkidu!' he mouthed. He walked slowly and stealthily into the hall, then crept to the back door, opened it quietly, turned and closed it. The latch clicked but the sound was drowned by the loud shouting of the baby.

As soon as Henry tried to grab Enkidu, the big cat leapt off the sill and bounded across the lawn.

'Enkidu!' Henry whispered as he gave chase.

Enkidu jumped over the gate. Henry opened it and ran through. The big cat waited while Henry closed the gate behind him. He found himself in a narrow, muddy lane. Enkidu immediately took off again, but at a more sedate pace. Henry trotted after him.

They were passing a patch of waste-ground between

Number Five and Number Four when Henry heard the heavy tramp of iron-studded boots. He stopped and glanced up at the road. The footsteps ceased. Curious to know where the henchmen had stopped, Henry crept through the long grass, dodging behind small bushes and leafless trees. Enkidu kept close to his heels.

At last Henry had a view of the gate to Number Five. Two henchmen stood before it, their faces concealed by their helmets. They were consulting a notebook. The man holding the notebook nodded and opened the gate. They marched up to the front door, and Henry heard the loud rat-tat of the door knocker. He caught the sound of a door opening, and a murmur of voices. The door closed.

The next moment Henry was startled to hear his name being called. All over the house. He saw the bedroom window open, and Mrs Reed lean out, shouting his name.

With sudden and chilling certainty Henry knew that Mrs Reed had not phoned the headmaster. She had called the henchmen. Why? Were they connected to the villains his aunt was so worried about? Was there no safety anywhere?

He couldn't return to Number Five. Ever.

'It's just you and me now, Enkidu,' Henry said quietly.

CHAPTER FOUR
The House in the Forest

Henry knew all about fear. When the shocking change to his life had occurred he had been so frightened he thought he would never recover. But he did, thanks to his cousin. Charlie had been crossing the great hall when Henry had arrived from the past, breathless, shocked and very scared. Charlie had hidden Henry. He had rescued and protected him, and then become his greatest friend. Henry wished Charlie was beside him now.

Mrs Reed was still calling Henry's name as he crept back to the lane. Once there, Enkidu took off again. This time the big cat sped away so fast Henry almost lost sight of him. The lane twisted and turned and Henry couldn't keep the flying ball of fur in sight. But he dared not call out. He came to a fork in the lane. On the left it carried on behind the houses, on the right a narrow track led into a dark wood.

Henry peered into the wood. He could see nothing

but giant trees, twisted moss-covered roots and fallen branches wrapped in ivy. Enkidu sat on the track, just inside the wood.

'Enkidu, are you sure about this?' asked Henry. He couldn't go back to the cafe. Henchmen might be lurking there.

The big cat turned and began to bound up the track. This time Henry didn't give chase. Wherever the track led, Enkidu obviously wanted him to follow. Henry paced slowly between the trees. If only he had found his aunt's note sooner. She must have written it when he was outside feeding Enkidu. He remembered she had straightened his anorak when she stood up to leave. Why couldn't she have told him what would happen? He wouldn't have protested. But then again, perhaps he would have done.

'Good day!' The voice was a shrill, strangled sound.

There was no one on the track ahead of him, or behind. 'Hullo!' said Henry.

'Toast and jam!' The sound floated in the air.

Henry looked up. A ghostly white shape dipped and hovered through the upper branches. He ran beneath it, his eyes never leaving the flying shape. The next moment he almost fell over Enkidu, who was also gazing at the white thing.

'A bird!' Henry declared, as the ghost came to rest on a branch above them.

A white bird. 'Ask where the white bird flies,' his aunt had told him.

'A thousand times good-night,' said the bird.

'A cockatoo!' Henry glanced at Enkidu. He seemed mesmerised by the bird.

'You were following it,' said Henry.

The cockatoo took off and they followed. Henry noticed that the trees around them were larger and darker. This was no wood. It was a forest. An ancient forest where small, unseen creatures moved through the shadows. He could hear a rustling, pattering, scuffling and, sometimes, a light flapping of wings.

A forest without end, thought Henry. He was in a foreign country, a timeless place. On they went, on and on into the darkness.

'You and me, and a cockatoo,' Henry told Enkidu and, in spite of their tricky situation, he smiled to himself.

At that moment he would have liked to rest on a welcoming pile of leaves, but the trees had begun to thin a little, and in the distance Henry could see tall wrought-iron gates. Beyond the gates there was a grey stone building with many steeply angled roofs and even a tower.

'Where have you brought me?' Henry muttered.

Enkidu ran to the gates.

There was nothing welcoming about the old

neglected-looking house but, for some reason, Henry felt drawn to it. He took a few paces towards the ornate rusted gates. A bell pull hung from a pillar on one side, its iron handle encrusted with lichen.

Henry went right up to the gates. He saw that part of the pattern at the top was formed from letters. There was a T, an L and an H. The other letters were rusted and misshapen but when Henry screwed up his eyes they became clearer. He made out a word, then another and another. An unmistakable name: 'The Littles' House'. And there was the white bird, perched on the porch roof.

Was this the place Pearl had meant him to come to? It looked deserted. What was he supposed to do now?

Before he could decide an ancient front door began to open. Even from the gate Henry could see the scratches and deep scars in the wood. He imagined soldiers kicking and battering the door in some long-ago battle.

There was a creaking and a shuddering, then a white-haired man appeared in the entrance. Henry found that he couldn't move. The man wore a white shirt, a long leather waistcoat and green velvet knee-breeches. He began to approach Henry along a mossy, paved walk. On either side thistles and tangled briars reached to the man's waist. He arrived at the gate and stared at Henry through the curling iron-work. He was short and wide and his face had a weathered tan. His eyes were a curious yellow, his lashes long and white.

'Spy or rover?' asked the man.

Henry stood his ground. 'If I was a spy I wouldn't tell you, would I?'

'Suit yourself.' The man turned away.

'Wait! Please!' begged Henry. 'I think my aunt wanted me to come here. I don't know why, but she wrote down the name. Look!' He held Pearl's note up to the gate.

'She's left off an s, and an apostrophe,' said the man.

'I can see that, but she was in a hurry,' said Henry.

'You were supposed to wait for Mr Lazlo,' said the man. 'He was detained for a time – a problem with the mayor.'

'I didn't find my aunt's note straight away, and then these children, the Reeds, said I should come home with them.'

'Dratted kids,' grunted the man. 'They did that to Flora, but we managed to get her out.' He reached under his waistcoat and unhitched a ring of heavy keys from his belt. Choosing the largest he pushed it into a lock in the centre of the gates and pulled one open. 'Come on, then,' he said to Henry. 'My name's

Herbert. I'm porter, handy-man, jack-of-all-trades and more.' He winked.

'I'm Henry, and . . .' Henry looked round for Enkidu but the black and white cat had leapt in from of him. The cockatoo flew into the open doorway calling, 'A plague on both your houses,' and Enkidu bounded after it.

'We can't have cats in here,' said Herbert. 'You'll have to get it out.'

Henry had no intention of getting Enkidu out of the house. If he was going in, then so was his cat. He followed Herbert up the path. When he reached the ancient, scarred door, he had a moment's doubt. But where else could he go?

'Get a move on.' Herbert spoke from the shadows beyond the door. 'You're letting the outside in.'

Nervously clenching his fists, Henry stepped over the threshold. He had the oddest sensation of moving backwards, not forwards. He shook his head, and hunched his shoulders as Herbert closed the door behind him. The air was filled with whispers.

Facing Henry, on the other side of a musty-smelling hallway, was a wide wooden staircase. It rose to a landing where a large gilt-framed mirror reflected nothing but dust. Henry's legs felt all at sea as the flagstones beneath his feet dipped into hollows and then rose unexpectedly.

A shaft of light brightened the hall as Herbert opened a door and proudly announced, 'The kitchen.'

Henry thought, *It's just a kitchen*. But as he stepped into the room he realised that it was not just a kitchen. It could better be described as an experience. The walls rose up and up until they reached a domed glass ceiling. The huge skylight was made of hundreds of topaz-coloured panes, giving the whole place the look of an old-fashioned photograph.

Below the ceiling two great oak beams ran the length of the room. They were hung with copper saucepans, cauldrons, bowls, ladles and other utensils the like of which Henry had never come across. They were all so far out of reach he wondered if anyone ever used them. And then he became aware of a step-ladder, the tallest he had ever seen, and almost at the top, a very, very tiny woman.

'Hullo!' the tiny person squeaked. 'You're late.'

'I know,' said Henry.

'Better late than never, eh?' said Herbert. 'Henry, meet Twig.'

'Are you hungry?' asked Twig.

'A bit,' Henry admitted.

Twig then did the most extraordinary thing. She leapt from the ladder, on to the top of a vast dresser. Every shelf was crammed with cracked and stained crockery, all piled higgledy-piggledy; plates balanced on bowls, cups teetering on one another. How it all stayed put was a mystery.

Bending over, Twig selected a large plate from the top shelf. Tucking this under one arm she bounced back on to the ladder, skimmed halfway down, and jumped on to the impossibly long table. It was only then that Henry saw the girl. She sat at the very end of the table. Behind her a window as wide and as tall as four doors rose above a giant stone sink. The girl's hair was as red as a flame. She was reading a book and took no notice of Henry whatsoever.

Twig ran across the table and peered into Henry's face. Her own was brown and leathery, but she had gentle dark eyes and a kind smile. She wore a long pink dress, a blue checked apron and furry slippers. Her brown hair was cut very short and her small pink ears were set unusually high on her head. The tip of her long nose was as active as a finger.

'Will eggs do?' Twig asked Henry.

'Eggs will do very well,' he said. He had eaten rather a lot of eggs recently, but one more wouldn't hurt, he reasoned, and he was very hungry again. He glanced at the red-haired girl and sat on a chair some distance from her.

'Ankaret, it would be nice if you could be polite for once,' Herbert said, throwing a disapproving look in the girl's direction.

She didn't respond.

'Perhaps she's deaf,' said Henry.

That did the trick. The girl looked up with a scowl. Her face was as pale as paper, her eyes were green and her nose and cheeks were covered in freckles. 'I happen to be reading a very interesting book,' she said, 'and I haven't got time for small-talk.'

Henry had never been one to give up easily. 'My name's Henry,' he said. 'I suppose yours is Ankaret. Unusual name, if you don't mind me saying.'

No response.

From the corner of his eye Henry had been watching Twig. In a matter of seconds she had shinned up the ladder, brought down a frying pan and rolled two eggs from under a chicken sitting in an old armchair. Now she was standing on a stool and frying the eggs in a peppery-smelling oil.

The stove crackled, the eggs sizzled and the topaz sunlight made the copper pans gleam. Henry felt almost at home.

At the very end of the room, half-hidden by the vast dresser, a door suddenly opened and a boy poked his head in. 'I smell eggs,' he said. 'Can I have one?' He came into the room and stood beside the stove.

'You've just had tea,' said Herbert.

'Have I?' The boy jerked his thumb at Henry.

'Who's he?'

'Why don't you ask him?' said Herbert.

'I'm Henry,' said Henry, before he could be asked.

'I'm Markendaya, or Mark,' the boy said solemnly.
'I come from India.' He was small and rather skinny.
'Are you the new rover?'

'I suppose so,' said Henry, without knowing what
it was.

'You were expected yesterday.' Mark came round
to Henry's side of the table and sat next to him. 'Did
you get lost?'

'I was hi-jacked,' Henry stated.

Mark emitted a knowledgeable grunt. 'That
happened to someone else.'

'What about you?' asked Henry. 'What did you –?'

'Don't!' Mark stood up and made for the door.
'Don't ask me,' he mumbled.' I don't want to talk
about it.' And then he was gone.

Herbert sighed and Twig tut-tutted.

Ankaret didn't even raise her head.

After a moment Henry asked, 'Did I say something
wrong?'

'He doesn't like to talk about his first life.' Twig
walked sedately across the table, carrying Henry's
plate of eggs. She set the plate before him and provided
him with a knife and fork. Henry assumed it must
be OK to walk on tables in this particular house. He

wondered what Pearl would have said. At least Twig's slippers looked reasonably clean.

There was a sudden loud shout from somewhere in the house. This was followed by several thumps on the staircase. The hanging pots and pans shivered and tinkled, but no one paid any attention.

Glancing nervously at the swinging pans above him, Henry thanked Twig for the eggs.

'You're welcome.' Twig dipped her head. Then she screamed.

It was such a shrill, heart-stopping sound, Henry dropped his knife and fork. Ankaret raised her head at last, and put her hands over her ears.

Twig was staring at something behind Henry and, looking round, he saw that Enkidu had appeared in the doorway.

'Cat! Cat!' shrieked Twig, pointing a trembling finger at Enkidu.

'Oh dear, I thought this might happen,' said Herbert. 'Twig, dear, stop screaming and we'll do something about it.'

'He's never hurt a soul,' said Henry. 'Never.'

Unconvinced, Twig retreated across the table, her eyes never leaving the big black and white cat. 'Out! Out! Out!' she screamed.

Enkidu seemed to consider this an invitation. He ran in and jumped on Henry's lap.

'GET IT OUT!' The voice behind Henry made him almost jump out of his chair. He turned to see a very tall man with a wiry black beard, and a navy-blue beret pulled over his curly black hair. He looked very like the man who had been standing outside Henry's window the night before.

'Cats are not allowed!' boomed the man, not bothering to introduce himself.

Henry decided to show the man some manners. He stood up, placing Enkidu on his chair. 'How do you do? I'm Henry,' he said pleasantly.

'I know who you are,' the man said irritably. 'Get that cat out of our house, out of our sight. Take it now, and make sure it never comes back.'

'I can't do that, sir,' Henry said firmly. 'Enkidu and I come together. If it wasn't for him, I might not be here at all.'

'Aargh!' growled the man. 'Didn't I make myself clear? Cats are taboo. They upset people. Take it OUT!'

'If my cat goes, then I go too,' said Henry, without even considering where he might go.

CHAPTER FIVE
Into the Tower

Several long, silent moments passed. Henry knew that he had said something foolish. Where *could* he go? At least he had Ankaret's attention. She was staring at him with interest.

Glowering at Henry, the bearded man said, 'Don't be stupid, boy! You're here now, and here you must stay until you have grown.'

'Grown?' This took Henry by surprise. 'I didn't know that I had come here to grow.'

'What else?' said the man. 'This is not an orphanage.'

Henry noticed Ankaret's shudder.

It was a chilling word: orphanage. In Henry's first life orphanages were spoken of in hushed tones. They were places to be avoided at all costs.

'My aunt didn't say anything about growing. I thought I was here to be safe.'

'And you will be when you have grown,' said the

man. 'Only then can you go home. Ankaret here was like you when she arrived, but now she is growing nicely, and will leave us very soon.'

Henry stared at Ankaret. 'Was it a marble?' he asked. 'Did it take you into the future? Away from your family and your life, and . . .' Henry's voice faltered because Ankaret had lifted her book in front of her face.

'There are other children like you here, Henry,' Herbert said kindly. 'They'll help you to understand.'

'Other children? Like me?' Henry was astonished. 'But how do we grow?'

'Are you going to put that cat out?' said Blackbeard, ignoring Henry's question.

'No,' said Henry. 'I don't care if I never grow. Enkidu is my life.'

The man looked perplexed. He frowned and scratched the back of his neck. The corners of his wide mouth tightened. Eventually, he said, 'It seems that I have misjudged you, Henry Yewbeam. My name is Mr Lazlo and, one way or another, I will make sure that you are allowed to grow.'

'How do you do?' said Henry, shaking Mr Lazlo's extended hand.

'You will soon understand why your cat is not welcome,' Mr Lazlo continued. 'Nevertheless it can stay with you in the tower, until it makes its first mistake.' He turned away, saying, 'Herbert, you'd better show him to the tower room.'

When Mr Lazlo had gone, Herbert said, 'The tower's not as bad as it sounds. Others have managed when necessary.'

'Necessary,' called the cockatoo, perched on a high saucepan. 'Necessary, very necessary.'

Enkidu jumped on the table and looked up at the bird. Henry pulled him off. Was that his cat's first mistake? The only parts of Twig that Henry could see were her small hands, clutching the edge of the table nearest to the stove. In a trembling voice she squeaked, 'Please, Herbert, take them to the tower now.'

'Let the boy eat his eggs first,' said Herbert.

Henry had lost his appetite. 'Enkidu likes eggs,' he said. 'Can I give them to him?'

'Go on then,' said Herbert disapprovingly.

Henry put his plate of eggs on the floor. Enkidu ate them rapidly. Henry returned the empty plate to the table, saying, 'Enkidu is very grateful.'

'That's as maybe,' Herbert said gruffly. 'Now it's to the tower for the pair of you.'

Henry and his cat followed the porter out of the kitchen and along a narrow passage. At the far end a low arch gave on to an ancient stairway. Weak light filtered down from a small window halfway up.

'You'll need a lantern tonight,' said Herbert. 'Up we go.' The porter led the way. Henry followed, while Enkidu crept uncertainly behind him. Every tread creaked, some of them even sank beneath the porter's large feet.

'Does anyone else sleep up here?' Henry tried not to sound anxious, but his voice betrayed him and came out a bit squeakier than he would have liked.

'Only when we have dangerous visitors,' said Herbert. 'Tonight you'll be alone.'

'Oh!'

'Shouldn't have brought your cat, should you?'

'I certainly should,' said Henry defiantly.

The stairs became darker and steeper. They twisted round and round, passing worm-eaten doors on shadowy landings. Up and up they went, reaching, at last, a dusty landing where Henry faced a small door with peeling blue paint and a rusty handle.

'Here we are,' said Herbert, showing Henry into a room with a sharply sloping ceiling.

There were two beds in the room, and signs of recent occupation: books on the floor, pencils, crayons and paper on a small table. Henry went to one of the beds and sat down. The springs twanged and the mattress was lumpy. Enkidu jumped up beside him.

'Pyjamas under the pillow,' said Herbert. 'Assorted garments in the cupboard.'

'Where's the bathroom?' asked Henry.

'Lavatory and wash-basin at the bottom of the stairs,' Herbert told him.

Henry hoped he wouldn't need the toilet in the night. 'It's a long way away,' he said.

'If you hadn't brought the cat,' said Herbert, 'you would have had a nice cosy bedroom and a big tiled bathroom with all mod cons.'

'Well, I did bring my cat,' Henry retorted, 'and I don't need mod cons, whatever they are.'

'Suit yourself.' Herbert turned to go.

Henry leapt up. 'I don't have to stay here until night-time, do I?'

'The cat does.' Herbert eyed Enkidu, who had made himself comfortable on the bed. 'And keep your door closed at night.'

'But what if he wants to go out?'

Herbert wrinkled his nose. He glanced at the cat. Enkidu's head rested on his paws and his eyes were closed. 'Then you'll have to take him out, won't you?'

Henry followed the porter out of the room, leaving the door ajar, just in case. As they descended the twisting staircase, Herbert suddenly stopped and, looking over his shoulder, he said, 'Perhaps you ought to know, Twig's husband was killed by a cat.'

Henry gasped. 'How?'

'How d'you think? Teeth and claws.'

48

'But . . .' Henry had never heard of a cat killing a person.

'The mayor's monster.' Herbert lowered his voice as he plodded round a corner. 'Luckily it was at night, so the mayor wasn't with his Dear One, as he calls it. No one comes here after dark.'

'No one?'

'They can't – forest keeps them away. The first henchmen who tried to enforce their curfew here were never seen again.'

'What happened to them?' Henry was intrigued.

'Who knows?' said Herbert. 'But no one ever tried again.' He descended a few more steps and then said, 'You're safe here, Henry. We're all Guardians.'

Henry thought about the forest and then he said quickly, 'Enkidu would never kill a person.'

'Depends on their size, doesn't it?' Herbert had a point. Twig was probably no taller than a kitten on its hind legs.

'Is . . . is Twig a . . . a . . .?' Henry didn't know quite how to put it.

'A person?' said Herbert, stepping down into the passage. 'Of course she is, as are the other little villains, as they used to be known. The Shaidi – forest people.' Herbert opened a door beside the arch. 'Your lavatory,' he said.

Henry looked into a dingy cupboard. The cracked

toilet didn't have a seat and one rusty tap dripped into a stained basin.

I've got things to do outside, now,' said Herbert, ushering Henry back to the kitchen. 'So entertain yourself until you hear the supper gong.' He strode out of a small back door and pulled it shut behind him.

The kitchen was deserted. There was no sign of Twig or Ankaret but several lamps burnt beneath copper shades hanging low over the table. The window-panes sparkled with amber light, the sky behind them darkening every second. Someone, somewhere, was singing. Henry walked round the never-ending table and opened the door into the hall. Now the voice was clearer. He climbed the stairs to the mirror hanging on the landing.

Here, the staircase divided into two, leading in opposite directions. Henry stood still, and listened.

Quiet voices moved through the air behind him. Henry swung round but there was no one there. He tried to shrug off the haunted feeling. The singing had stopped. He trod cautiously up the left-hand set of stairs, hoping the singing would begin again. When he reached the top he could hear a gentle hum.

Following the sound, Henry made his way towards a lantern standing on a small table at the end of a long corridor. The gentle humming issued from a door that stood slightly ajar. Henry pulled it a little and peeped in.

In the centre of a candlelit room, a girl with golden hair was slowly spinning. Round and round she went, humming in a delightfully tuneful way. Henry was not usually affected by dancing girls and musical humming, but this girl was so graceful, her flying hair so soft and bright, he felt quite overcome, and could only stand in the open doorway and gape. He was too entranced to notice a movement round the girl's legs, a dusty whirl and whirr, a scamper, a squeak and a gasp.

The girl came to a standstill, swaying a little. 'Oh,' she said. 'Whoo! I feel a bit dizzy.' She sank quickly into a pink armchair.

Henry said, 'Hi!' But he remained in the doorway, unable to utter another word, which was unusual for him.

'Come in,' said the girl. 'You're Henry, aren't you?'

'Yes.' Henry took a cautious step into the room.

'I'm Marigold.' She beamed. 'They told me all about you – and your cat. Oh dear!'

This remark untied Henry's tongue. 'What d'you mean, oh dear?' He shut the door and walked towards the girl.

'Don't get me wrong,' said Marigold quickly. 'I like cats. It's just . . .'

'I know,' sighed Henry. 'A cat killed Twig's husband.'

He thought he heard a small grumbling sound, but continued, 'All cats aren't the same, you know.'

'Of course they aren't.' Marigold smiled at Henry. 'Let's change the subject. Tell me how you came to be a rover.'

Henry frowned. 'Why are we called rovers?'

'We are trying to find the right place – that's what Herbert says, like arrows, looking for their mark. But for now we are rovers because we are lost.'

Henry didn't like that description. He sat on the pink quilt that covered Marigold's bed, hoping she would tell him her story.

'So when did it begin?' prompted Marigold. 'What happened in your first life?'

'It was nearly a hundred years ago,' said Henry warily.

'I believe you.' Marigold gave him a reassuring grin. 'Mine was two hundred years ago.'

They stared at each other and began to laugh.

'It's a good thing we don't look that old.' Marigold sank back into the chair, still giggling.

'It was a marble,' Henry said when his laughter had subsided and he found himself plunging into the story of the event that changed his life. It had remained in his head so vividly he had no trouble in recounting it.

Marigold sat very still and silent, while Henry told her how, on the coldest night in living memory he had been playing marbles. 'We were staying with my uncle, my brother and me, because our sister was very ill. My uncle ran a school in an old, old house. The students had all gone home, and I thought the great hall would be the best place to play. I'd just had a row with our cousin, Ezekiel. He was older than us, and a real horror.' Henry couldn't suppress a shudder when he mentioned Ezekiel's name. 'I kept finishing puzzles for him, he was hopeless, and I think that he hated us because he had a miserable home life, and we were always so happy.'

Marigold grimaced sympathetically.

'I thought I was alone in the hall,' Henry went on, 'but then this marble came rolling towards me; a huge marble. I picked it up.'

Marigold leant forwards. 'Yes,' she breathed. 'Just like I did. And you looked into it.'

'It was so amazing.'

'Cities of gold, shining rivers, rainbows, forests, silver mountains . . .?'

'Yes, yes.' Henry nodded vehemently. 'It was incredible, travelling through the world like that, so fast, feeling the sun, the rain, the snow, and then, suddenly, I was back where I began, and staring at a boy who looked like me. It was weird. I discovered

53

that he was my distant cousin, or rather my great-great-nephew, Charlie, and I'd travelled into the future, into now. But I was in the very same place and . . . this was the really awful part . . . ' Henry paused for effect.

'Yes?' urged Marigold, on the very edge of her seat.

'Ezekiel was still alive, still at the school, still out to get me. Over a hundred years old and still hating me. Of course it made it even worse that I hadn't aged. He'd rolled the marble, you see, hoping I would vanish into the Ice Age, or something worse.'

Marigold gasped. 'Appalling.'

Henry wasn't able to tell her how Ezekiel and his grandson, Manfred, had pursued him, caught him and half-buried him, because, at that moment, the door opened, just a crack, and Ankaret looked in.

'I didn't know you were here.' Ankaret frowned at Henry.

'He's just told me about his roving,' said Marigold. 'Come in and tell him what happened to you, Ankaret.'

'No.' Ankaret withdrew her head and closed the door.

'Why's she like that?' asked Henry.

'She's afraid to go back,' Marigold told him.

'Go back? You mean . . .? But we can't go back. My aunt was always telling me that the gap we left behind would be closed; our families would remember us, but their lives couldn't be changed to . . . to fit us in again.' Henry used to feel desperate when he thought about this, but, with Charlie's help, he had accepted it, and now felt happy in the present.

'Returning to our first lives is out of the question,' Marigold agreed. 'No, I mean our second lives. You want to go back there, don't you?'

'Of course.'

'Me too. But Ankaret's second life is so awful, she'd rather stay here.'

'Well, it could be worse.' Henry looked round Marigold's bright and cheerful room. 'Twig cooked me some eggs. And Herbert's OK. The kitchen is warm . . .'

'Henry!' Marigold's deep blue eyes fixed on his with urgent intensity. 'It's not safe here.'

Henry swallowed. 'What d'you mean?'

'I mean we can't go out, and sometimes we must hide. If the mayor found us here, he would want to know who we were and why we came in. But this is the only place in the world where we can grow. As soon as we do, we'll be safe and can leave. But then the mayor will want to know how. Because he can't, you see; he will never get out. No one can, unless the Shaidi help them. People have tried, so I'm told. Some never recover from the attempt.'

He remembered Peter's remark about the ghostly-looking people: 'They tried to get through.' *Through what? That sinister stone arch?*

'My aunt got out,' he said, hopefully.

'Must have been the equinox.' Marigold gave a knowing smile. 'If you come in on the equinox, you can leave. But only if you go within the hour.'

'Oh.' It was beginning to make sense.

'You can come in any time,' Marigold explained, 'if you can find the place. Few do. Someone brought me to the arch, six weeks ago and . . .'

Marigold was interrupted by a loud sneeze. It seemed to come from under the bed Henry was sitting on.

Marigold grinned. 'You might as well come out, Mint,' she said. 'Henry's cat isn't here.'

Henry bent over and stared into the shadows beneath Marigold's bed. A tawny face emerged; its eyes were round and sparkling. A boy crawled out. Was it a boy? He was so very small, probably only a foot high, but he was certainly not a baby. He had Twig's features: the long nose, the small ears set high on the head, the soft, fuzzy hair and thin mouth. He wore a green checked shirt, brown velveteen trousers and yellow boots.

'This is Twig's son, Mint,' said Marigold. 'Mint, meet Henry.'

Mint screwed up his long nose and rushed out of

the room. As soon as he had gone, a tiny girl, quite clearly related to Mint, crawled from under the bed and, with a loud squeal, ran for the door. She was gone in a flash of red skirts and emerald green boots.

'Marjoram,' Marigold told Henry. 'She's scared at the best of times, but now, with your cat about, she's in a real state.'

'My cat has never . . .' Henry paused, remembering a certain smelly rat and a greedy mouse. 'Well, hardly ever, hurt a thing.'

Marigold shrugged. 'It's no good telling them. They're fatherless.' She jumped up, suddenly. 'I'm going to give you a tour, so you know where everything is. Someone did it for me. It helps you to settle in before it's time to fly home.'

'Fly?' said Henry.

'It's the only way, when you think about it. Tomorrow, it's my turn.'

'You're going back?' Henry was disappointed. He liked Marigold's company.

'I'm ready,' she said. 'I've grown two inches in six weeks. What d'you think of that?'

Henry didn't know what to think. He followed Marigold round the vast, echoing, draughty house. They climbed shadowy stairways, squeezed through tiny secret doors, made their way down dimly lit passages and trod across bright Turkish carpets. And every now and again Henry would hear the distant whispering voices, but he didn't like to mention it.

'Herbert is trying to light every corner of the house,' said Marigold, 'but it's a bit of a challenge.'

'I can see that,' said Henry, stumbling down a hidden step.

'He's a bit obsessed with fire,' Marigold went on. 'They all are.'

'All?' Henry wondered who else he would meet in the house.

'Miss Notamoth, Mrs Hardear and Professor Pintail. Sometimes I've seen them all cosy round a fire and muttering a strange jumble of sounds.'

Henry wasn't sure he wanted to meet them after all.

When Marigold had decided that Henry had seen everything he needed to see, she said, 'There's someone we must visit now.'

They had reached a splendid highly polished door with a row of carved birds flying across the lintel at the top.

Marigold knocked.

No answer.

She knocked again. 'It's me, Princess – Marigold.'

'Princess?' Henry exclaimed in a harsh whisper.

Marigold whispered, 'She says she is.'

'Yes?' came a soft voice.

Marigold opened the door and Henry followed her into a room that smelt of mothballs and lavender. It could best be described as a rather untidy library.

The princess, if that's what she was, reclined on a faded velvet-covered ottoman. A large oil lamp, standing on a chest behind her, gave the elderly princess the look of a tragic heroine in a painting. She was dressed entirely in black and her face looked as fragile as an egg. She had stringy, shoulder-length grey hair and a thin fringe above mild grey eyes. The only regal things about her were her fingers, which were covered in rings. They sparkled hypnotically, even on her thumbs. Henry couldn't take his eyes off them. When the princess raised her hand he wondered how such a frail person could lift such weighty brilliance.

'Sit down, angels.' The princess had a pleasant, chiming sort of voice.

Marigold sat on a large armchair, facing the ottoman. She patted the gap beside her and Henry carefully squeezed in. There was nowhere else to sit, except for the floor, which was littered with books. Even the walls appeared to have been constructed entirely out of books. You could hardly see the shelves, they were so stuffed with manuscripts, paperbacks, hardbacks, ancient tomes and ragged leather folders.

'Another rover,' said the princess, revealing a row of rather uneven teeth.

Henry returned her smile and nodded, 'I'm Henry.'

'So, Henry.' The princess laced her ringed fingers together. 'There are things that you should know.'

'There certainly are,' Henry agreed.

'To begin with, you must never leave the house. You mustn't be seen by anyone from the town.'

'I have been seen –' Henry began.

'Not here,' the princess said sharply. 'No one knows that you are here. They must never know. The Shaidi – little villains, they call them – the Shaidi have agreed to help lost children on the understanding that they themselves remain a secret. If anyone knew that Twig and her family were here, they would be hunted down and killed.'

'Killed?' said Henry in a shocked voice. 'Why?'

'It's a long story.' The princess pressed a hand to her stomach. 'And I believe it will soon be time for supper.'

'Please!' Henry leant forwards. 'Tell me about the little villains.'

'Tell him, princess,' Marigold begged, 'so that he understands.'

'They are not villains for a start,' said the princess. 'Their name is the Shaidi, and they were here long, long before anyone else came to the forest. They are the spirit of the trees, the heartbeat, you could say.' The princess twisted a bright ring on her little finger.

'A hundred years ago, a band of criminals came to hide with their families in the forest. They were thieves, ruffians, murderers, scum of the earth. They buried their vast, stolen treasure – gold and jewels worth millions. And then they began to cut and burn the forest. The Shaidi's home. The Shaidi tried to stop them; they stole the axes, blew out the flames, stung the strangers with arrows, made their food rotten and their milk sour. They made things vanish. They were given a name, little villains, and then they were killed with guns; weapons they had never encountered.'

A thread of ice stole down Henry's spine. 'But not all of them,' he said.

'All but a few. Twig and her family are the last of their kind.'

Henry thought of the cat that had killed Twig's husband, and he said, slowly, 'I understand.'

Marigold touched his hand. 'Not everything, Henry. You don't understand everything, yet.'

'Indeed.' The princess smiled. 'Before they finally gave up, the Shaidi made one last, wonderful spell. They called on the forest to defend itself, and it did. Trees and rocks, bushes and plants coiled and curved, looped and twined, stretched and swelled until a great a barrier was formed, enclosing Timeless in an area that no one can ever leave. A punishment, if you like. The Shaidi knew that the effort of making such a great spell would weaken them, and it did, but now the forest can never be destroyed.' She thought a moment and added, 'There was a tiny flaw in the Shaidi's calculations. The matter of six lost hours on every equinox.' She laughed and clapped her hands. 'I expect you were surprised to find morning so close on the heels of midnight.'

'Yes,' Henry murmured, 'but it didn't seem to bother my aunt.' Suddenly he badly wanted to see her again, and be in the little white house on the cliff.

'Of course, she knew.' The princess raised her twinkling fingers.

The glitter of rings was beginning to get to Henry. He often sneezed in bright sunlight. Now his sneeze was explosive. A pile of books fell off a high shelf behind him, bringing down a cloud of dust.

Both children leapt up, dust in their eyes and mouths, fragments of grimy paper, dead flies and cobwebs covering their arms and shoulders. They patted their heads and faces, and tried to brush the sticky webs and dead things off their shoulders. When they could safely open their eyes, they saw that the princess was smiling at them.

'I know what's up there now,' said the princess. 'I'll have to get Twig in here with her duster.'

'And a ladder,' Marigold suggested.

A sound could be heard, distant and deep. Henry

wondered if this was the supper gong.

The princess swung her legs off the ottoman, exclaiming, 'Food. You can take me into supper. We'll have another little chat later, Rover Henry. But right now, I'm dying for my supper. I do hope it will be something with legs.'

CHAPTER SIX
The Mayor and his Monster

The princess walked remarkably fast for an elderly person. The children could hardly keep up with her as she sped along corridors, down the stairs and across the wide hall. She reached the kitchen at least a minute before them.

Just as Marigold was about to push open the door, Henry whispered, 'What did she mean, "something with legs"?'

'Twig finds things to eat in the garden,' Marigold explained. 'They don't always have legs.'

'Fish?' Henry said, hopefully.

'The river's not exactly outside the door. I mean snails and stuff.'

'Stuff?' Henry thought of things that slid and wriggled.

'Twig's a great cook,' said Marigold reassuringly, as she led him past the stove to the place where he'd eaten before.

By the time he sat down Henry wasn't sure he wanted any supper.

The princess had settled herself at the head of the table. Behind the old lady the enormous window blazed with reflected light. Henry, far away at the opposite end, could barely make her out. But he could see that Herbert and Mr Lazlo sat on either side of her. Next to Mr Lazlo was a red-faced woman with tufty brown hair and very large purple-coloured ears.

'Mrs Hardear,' Marigold whispered, when she saw Henry staring at the woman. 'Can you believe it?'

Henry grinned.

The kitchen was filling up. A woman with smooth brown hair clinging to her scalp floated over to a chair close to the stove. She wore a lacy grey cardigan with wide sleeves that looked like wings, and horn-rimmed spectacles that made her brown eyes look huge.

'Miss Notamoth,' Marigold said in an undertone.

Ankaret took a seat opposite Henry and a tall girl with dark ringlets sat at the end of the table between Ankaret and Marigold. Mark slipped in beside Henry, and then a boy who looked like a large cherub hauled out a chair beside Ankaret and sank into it with a long 'Ahhh' of pleasure.

'What's on the menu today, then?' said the cherub.

'Cats' tails,' said Ankaret, darting a look at Henry.

'That's a new one,' said the cherub. 'Ah, here it comes.'

At the far end of the table Twig placed a bowl of steaming soup before the princess. The contents of the bowl held an uncanny radiance, for a soft glow lit the princess's features. With a smile of pleasure, she daintily dipped her spoon into the bowl and, lifting it to her mouth, she swallowed the contents with a noisy slurp. Pronouncing the soup excellent, the princess added, 'Twig, you have outdone yourself.'

Twig gave a little skip of pleasure, accidentally knocking a large peppermill across the table.

The cherub gave a hoot of laughter and called out, 'Well done, Twig.'

Twig was now busy serving Mr Lazlo and Mrs Hardear. The bowls looked almost too big for her tiny arms, but she seemed to enjoy her task. Next came Herbert and the cherub. She gave the cherub the biggest smile Henry had yet seen on her small, leathery face. The cherub was obviously a favourite.

'Cook's pet,' muttered Ankaret.

Mark nudged Henry and rolled his eyes. 'Ankaret is never happy,' he whispered.

The girl with ringlets leant forwards and said, hesitantly, 'I'm Lucy. Pleased to meet you, Henry. I . . . I hope you'll be . . . you'll be lucky.'

Henry frowned. He was about to ask what Lucy meant when Twig walked down the table and placed a bowl of soup in front of him. He noticed that her boots were muddy but decided not to mention it. No one else appeared to mind. Perhaps they were just glad to get a meal.

Henry picked up his spoon and looked eagerly into the bowl of steaming, greenish soup.

'Leek and potato, I would say,' said Marigold. 'Yummy.'

A few specks of very fine dust dropped into Henry's bowl. He looked up at the wide beam far above him. A large cauldron swung very gently. It blocked his view of whatever might have been lying on top of the beam. He thought he saw a tiny hand. But no, he must have been mistaken.

Henry tasted the soup. It was good, hot but a bit unusual. He took a second spoonful. Not so good. 'Urgh!' he declared. His voice echoed up into the sea of shining pans hanging above him. Following the strange sound his voice made he looked up, and saw Mint, standing with his legs apart, his hands on his hips. The tiny boy was grinning down at Henry.

The room tilted. Faces became pale blurs. Henry's stomach was on fire. His head felt as though several hammers were beating on it. He slumped forwards, his face met the hot liquid and he passed out.

When he woke up, he was lying on his bed. Enkidu was standing on his chest, gazing at him with concern. Henry's stomach churned. He thought he was going to be sick and sat up quickly.

How long have I been asleep? Henry wondered. *An hour? Two hours?* It was light outside. And then he remembered the poisonous soup, and Mint standing on the beam above him, a gleeful smile on his long, brown face.

'He poisoned me,' Henry murmured. 'Did he want to kill me because of you, Enkidu?'

The big cat purred. The wrong response, Henry thought.

There was a knock on the door. Henry wondered what to expect. 'Y-e-s?' he said weakly.

The door opened and the cherub's face appeared.

'Brought you some breakfast,' said the cherub. 'It's way past breakfast time, but we thought you might not manage any more – just yet. Name's Christian, by the way.'

'Breakfast,' said Henry. 'When did I have supper?'

'Yesterday.' The cherub entered, bearing a tray of toast, roasted mushrooms and a glass of milk. 'Mr Lazlo carried you up here last night.'

'Did he?' Henry rubbed his eyes.

The cherub carefully placed the tray on a chair beside Henry's bed. 'I haven't known the little villains – which they can be when they're upset – I haven't known them be so angry since their father was murdered. I see they've given you the full treatment.'

He stared at Henry's head.

Henry put up a hand and felt his forehead. The skin was smooth, not rough and warty. He had thought he might have been turned into a toad. His hair was coarser than he remembered, but it was still there.

The cherub shook his head, smiling ruefully. 'It's green, Henry. Your hair's gone green. I heard they can do that, but I've never seen it before.'

Henry glared at the cherub. He tugged a few hairs from the top of his head. Their vivid colour made him gasp. 'Why?' he cried. 'What did I do to make them so . . . so mean?'

The cherub looked sympathetic. 'They're frightened, Henry. They're the last of their line and they believe that your cat is going to finish them off. No more Shaidi, no more plant magic, no protection for the trees, no help for rovers. Imagine.'

Henry frowned at the strands of green hair lying in his palm. He looked at Enkidu curled peacefully at his feet. How could he prove that his friend was not a killer? Not a killer of people, however small. He took a piece of toast and bit into it. He didn't feel like eating mushrooms.

'I promise the mushrooms haven't been tampered with,' said the cherub with a grin.

'I don't want them,' Henry said grumpily.

'I'll look out for you, Henry. In a few days your

hair will be brown again. So cheer up.' The cherub went to the door. 'See you later.'

A thought occurred to Henry. 'Christian,' he said.

The cherub waited at the door.

'Were you time-twisted through a marble? And did it make you stop growing?'

Christian nodded.

'How old were you?'

The cherub shrugged. 'A hundred and fifty years ago, I was nine.'

'But you've grown – a lot.'

'I'm the right size for thirteen, thanks to the Shaidi. My dad was very large.' He grinned and opened the door.

'Wait, please.'

The cherub sighed impatiently and fiddled with the door knob.

'You've grown but you haven't gone home.'

'I'm very glad I've grown,' said Christian, 'because my brain has acquired much in four years, and my mind has aged. I'd feel silly if I was still small. My journey failed because my heart wasn't in it.' The cherub turned and gave Henry a rather forced smile. 'You mustn't worry. If you really want to get home, you will.'

'Didn't you want to go home?'

'No.' The cherub opened the door and went out.

Why? For the first time it struck Henry that he might never see Charlie or Pearl again.

'Are we going to be stuck here forever?' Henry pulled Enkidu closer.

There was a grinding roar from outside, soon followed by the hollow sound of a large bell.

Enkidu leapt off the bed and ran to a small table under the window. Jumping on to the table he stared down into the garden. What he saw there made him pull back his ears and emit a soft growl.

Henry got out of bed and joined Enkidu at the window. He had a good view of the overgrown path and the rusting iron gates. Behind the gates stood a figure. It wore a wide-brimmed hat the colour of charcoal, and carried something on its shoulder: a huge bundle, as grey as an angry cloud. Three henchmen stood behind the stranger, their faces hidden behind sinister helmets.

For a few seconds Henry was too intrigued to move. The man's face was almost as ashen as his eyes. He had a drooping sour-milk moustache, a long, bony chin and a thin, pointed nose. A few strands of colourless hair stuck out from under his hat.

But it was the creature on the man's shoulder that had really caught Henry's attention. He blinked, hoping to rid himself of the dreadful image. Was it his imagination? No, it was real. The creature was almost a cat but twice the size. One of its eyes glared furiously up at Enkidu, the other eye was a line of stitches; both of its ears were torn and ragged, and a long scar ran from its stitched eyelids, across its nose and down to its bearded chin.

Henry leapt away from the window just as the man looked up.

'Enkidu, come away!' Henry whispered fiercely.

Enkidu's growls gained strength. He was practically roaring.

Henry bent low and dragged Enkidu off the table.

'He must have seen you,' moaned Henry. 'Maybe he saw me. Now what?'

Quickly he got dressed. He was about to rush out of the door when it opened and Marigold burst in, her face flushed, her golden hair flying.

'So this is where you sleep,' Marigold said breathlessly, flinging herself on Henry's bed.

Before Henry could open his mouth, Ankaret ran in, dragging Mark behind her. 'Oh!' Ankaret looked round the room. 'This is our place on a Tuesday.'

'Well, it's mine now,' said Henry. 'I thought you all had nice, bright rooms on the other side of the house.'

'Not on a Tuesday when the mayor comes to the house,' said Marigold. 'He has a regular appointment with Mr Lazlo. and he'll be here any moment. We need to hide here until he leaves. By the way, your hair is green.'

'I know,' snapped Henry. 'Anyway, the mayor just saw me, or at least I think it was the mayor. He had a monster cat.'

'What?' cried the girls.

'How did he see you?' asked Mark in a wobbly voice.

'Enkidu went to the window and growled,' Henry explained. 'I followed him, and this man looked up. So did his cat. He might not have seen me, but he definitely saw Enkidu.'

'Oh no!' Ankaret glared accusingly at Henry. 'We'll have to find somewhere else to hide. Right now!'

'I know where!' Marigold was already out of the door.

The others followed her, past more battered, dusty doors and up winding stairways that seemed to have no end. They were going round in circles for it was, of course, a tower. At length they came to a narrow, flimsy-looking ladder propped against the wall. Two of its rungs were missing. In the ceiling directly above it there was a small trapdoor.

'The attic!' Marigold turned and gave them all an encouraging smile.

'It's very small,' Ankaret said doubtfully.

'And the door could be heavy,' added Henry. 'Have you been up there before, Marigold?'

'Not exactly. But I noticed the ladder one day when I was exploring.'

Henry had an idea. He smiled at Enkidu, sitting at his feet. 'How about it, Enkidu?' Henry looked up at the trapdoor and nodded at it. 'What d'you think?'

Enkidu slipped past the children, skimmed up the ladder and nudged the door with his head. It fell open with a bang.

'Just like a dog,' said Marigold admiringly.

'Impressive,' Ankaret admitted. 'Now what? The cat's much lighter than we are.'

Enkidu had disappeared into the attic.

'I could go first,' Mark offered. 'I'm the lightest.'

No one objected.

Mark gripped the sides of the ladder and stepped on to the first rung. He looked round at everyone and grinned nervously.

'Well done,' said Marigold.

'Go on,' said Ankaret impatiently.

Mark began to climb. His skinny legs shook and he kept giving little gasps and yelps, especially when he had to stretch his legs over a missing rung. But, eventually, he pulled himself to the top and crawled into the hole.

'Hurrah!' cried Marigold.

'Shh!' Henry was sure he had heard a voice beneath them.

Marigold clapped a hand over her mouth.

Someone was climbing the tower steps. Now there were two voices and the tramp, tramp of two pairs of feet.

'Quick! Quick!' whispered Marigold, throwing herself up the rickety ladder. Ankaret followed her. Henry started climbing before Ankaret had reached the top. A rung cracked under his foot and he dropped back to the ground.

'Shh!' hissed Ankaret.

Henry began again, gingerly hauling himself over the gaps in the ladder, and trying not to break any more rungs. At last he pulled himself into the dark and musty attic. He squatted for a moment at the edge of the hole, dizzy and breathless from his frantic climb.

Splinters of light filtered through the cracks in the roof tiles, and he could see the others crouching on wide, rough planks, their shoulders hunched against the dark shapes on the beams above them.

'We'll have to bring the ladder up,' Henry whispered. 'They might see it, and wonder if anyone is up here.'

'But they'll hear us,' Marigold squeaked.

This was true. Henry stared at three pairs of frightened eyes. What could be done? He was about to close the trapdoor and hope for the best, when Enkidu took control of the situation.

With a sudden, silent leap the big cat landed on the beam above them. There was a deafening screech, a wild flapping, and black feathers flew in all directions as a crowd of birds took off. A family of jackdaws had been happily wintering in the tower until Enkidu landed in their midst.

For a few seconds the birds sped round the attic, crashing against beams, shrieking and squawking, until one of them saw the exit.

'Now!' said Ankaret. 'Pull up the ladder, while the birds are making a racket.'

Henry bent over and grabbed the top rung. He heaved. As the ladder came up the others moved it across the attic space. The birds were now diving through the opening. Wings beat in Henry's face, half-blinding him, talons tore across his fingers. One of his hands was so painful he lost his grip, but he clung on with the other. Grasping the ladder with two hands, once again, he kept going until the ladder was in the attic. It was too long to lie on the floor; they had to prop it at an awkward angle, wedged between a floorboard and the sloping roof.

Henry closed the trapdoor and sat back.

The clatter of birds made it impossible to hear any voices or footsteps, but gradually the noise subsided and the tower was silent. Someone must have helped the birds fly out through the back door.

How long would they have to wait before it was safe to leave the attic? Henry was about to speak when he heard the footsteps again. Up the stairs they came, tramp, tramp, tramp. The two voices were raised. It sounded like an argument. One voice definitely belonged to Mr Lazlo, the other was pitched higher but louder. It grumbled and whined in a grim, bullying tone. And it was getting closer.

Marigold's eyes were wide with alarm. She mouthed the word, 'Mayor.'

CHAPTER SEVEN
Hiding in the Attic

Henry clasped Enkidu tight, and stared at the trapdoor.

The two men were now immediately below the attic, their words quite distinct.

'What's up there?' the mayor demanded.

'Bats,' said Mr Lazlo.

'Only bats?' The mayor sounded suspicious. 'Not cats?'

'Cats can't fly, Enoch. How would a cat get up there?'

'You tell me. You won't allow my Dear One in the house, because of that woman's wretched allergy to cat fur, but I saw one. A large long-haired creature, white blob on its nose, white chest, white paws. It was yowling at my Dear One.'

'*That woman*, as you call her,' snapped Mr Lazlo, 'is my mother. She has the delicate constitution of a Moringian princess.'

'If you say so,' said the mayor. 'Nevertheless, I saw a CAT!'

Mr Lazlo sighed. 'I'm sorry, Enoch. But, as you have seen for yourself, it's nowhere in this tower.'

'Flew out of the window, did it?'

'I've no idea,' Mr Lazlo couldn't disguise his impatience. 'We'd better start your treatment, or you'll be going home in the dark, and you know how dangerous that is.'

The mayor gave a guttural snarl. 'Trees. Give me the creeps. What's in the forest, Lazlo? Are you going to tell me one day?'

Mr Lazlo gave a half-hearted laugh. 'I'm as much in the dark as you are.'

'Huh!' grunted the mayor.

The two men moved off, their footsteps gradually receding as they descended the ancient stairway. But even when the thumps and creaks could be heard no more, the children in the attic remained silent.

Curiosity overcame Henry at last. 'Why does the mayor come here for treatment?' he whispered.

'He has a metal heart,' Marigold told him in a low voice.

'And a metal shoulder,' Mark added. 'He wears the killer cat on it to keep out the cold.'

'But it's not enough,' said Marigold, 'and sometimes the mayor howls with pain. Mr Lazlo is the only one who knows how to treat his condition.'

'But it's the Shaidi who make the balm,' said

Ankaret. 'And the Shaidi who work through the night, pounding and mixing and shaking and sniffing. They took me to their work-room once, when I couldn't sleep.'

Henry had never seen Ankaret so animated. She must have been very impressed by the Shaidi, he thought, to allow herself to talk so much. To his surprise, Ankaret had more to say.

'The mayor loves his treatment.' Ankaret grimaced and screwed up her eyes. 'He sits there, moaning with pleasure, while Mr Lazlo's big hands pummel and smooth his horrible white skin, with all its puckered purple scars. Herbert says he got the scars from a bear, or something like it, that attacked him in the forest.'

'Ankaret, how did you see all that?' said Marigold.

Henry wondered about the bear.

'Where were you?' asked Mark, frowning. 'Weren't you scared?'

Ankaret shrugged. 'I looked through a crack in the floorboards. I wanted to know why the mayor didn't interfere down here in the forest. Herbert said that life in the town was bad: henchmen parading with their clubs, curfews, no clocks allowed, and the people are sad and sullen, except for the favoured few.'

'Like the Reeds,' said Marigold.

'A girl called Flora was kidnapped by the Reeds,' said Ankaret, 'like you were, Henry.'

Before Henry could ask what happened to Flora, there was a thump on the trapdoor.

Everyone in the attic tensed. Ankaret put a hand over her mouth. They had forgotten to whisper.

'It's only me,' said a familiar voice. 'Are you all OK?'

Henry opened the trapdoor and looked down at Christian's smiling face. 'Can we come out?'

'Not safe yet,' said Christian, brandishing a broom. 'The henchmen are looking for your cat.'

'He's up here,' said Henry.

Christian grinned. 'You'd better stay where you are until you hear them go.' He waved a hand and left.

Henry shut the trapdoor. 'Christian is very . . .' He searched for the right word.

'Thoughtful,' Marigold supplied. 'He was a choirboy. Not that all choirboys are thoughtful. He doesn't have to hide, nor does Lucy. They've been here for ages. They've grown a lot since they came and the mayor thinks they're part of the princess's family.'

'So what happened to Christian in his first life?' asked Henry.

'He was in church, putting out the hymn books,' said Marigold, 'and a marble rolled out in the aisle, right in front of him. Christian said it must have come from one of the pews, but they were all empty. He said the light from the stained-glass window made the marble shine so fiercely he could barely look at it.'

'You can't leave a thing like that on the ground, can you?' said Ankaret with feeling.

'So he picked it up and looked into it.' Henry lowered his voice and glanced at Mark. 'And travelled.'

'Poor Christian,' said Marigold. 'The next thing he knew he was being dragged out of the church by a horrible warden who thought he'd come to steal the church silver. He was taken to the police station, but they didn't believe him when he said he was the son of Oliver and Ottoline Ottershaw, because they'd been in their graves for more than ninety years.'

'So how did he get here?' asked Henry.

'The police tried to find out where Christian came from,' Marigold continued, 'but of course they couldn't, and nothing Christian said made sense. No one had reported him missing, so he was fostered. But his foster parents were very unkind, and when Christian kept talking about the choir and his family, they locked him in his room, and he felt too sick to eat.'

Ankaret said quietly, 'He was called a liar and a fraud, over and over and over.'

'Like you were,' said Marigold.

Ankaret was silent. She hung her head and drummed her fingers on her knees.

'A woman called Treasure found him,' Marigold went on. 'She found me, too, and Ankaret.' She glanced at Mark and added softly, 'And Mark.'

Henry was astonished. This Treasure had to be Pearl's sister. Was she gifted with a magical talent for seeking out children in danger? She was distantly related to Charlie, and he had an unimaginable talent. He came from that sort of family. Henry's family. Not that Henry was gifted in any way.

Marigold broke into his thoughts, saying, 'I'm going home tonight!'

'Where you'll be happy,' Ankaret said flatly.

'You next, I suppose,' Henry said cheerfully, looking at Ankaret.

'You suppose wrong,' snapped Ankaret. 'Haven't you learnt anything? You heard Christian's story. No everyone's second life is good. Some of us are shut out of happiness forever.'

Chastened, Henry turned away from Ankaret's pale, angry face. He could think of nothing to say. He wanted to apologise but decided that it would only make matters worse. Mark was muttering sadly to himself in the dark, and all the fun of hiding away in a dusty attic suddenly evaporated.

They sat in silence for a while, glancing at each other now and again. Henry wanted to know about Marigold's second life. She had been happy, until someone noticed she wasn't growing. Who were these people who spied on children who hadn't grown, and how did Treasure manage to rescue them before they were stolen away?

Henry's thoughts whirled in his head. He felt very tired, even though he'd slept for so long. The effects of the poisonous dust still hadn't worn off. He closed his eyes, his head drooped and he fell asleep. He was woken up by a bang and a loud roaring.

Henry's eyes flew open. He sat bolt upright and stared into the darkness. 'What's that?'

'Motorbikes,' said Marigold. 'The mayor and his henchmen are leaving.'

'Did he take his cat?' asked Henry, thinking of the evil single eye.

'Who knows?' said Marigold lightly. 'Let's get out of here.'

Henry lifted up the trapdoor and they pushed the ladder through the opening.

Ankaret was the first to climb down. 'Let's hope we never have to do that again,' she said, jumping to the floor.

The others followed, carefully. Henry came last, not forgetting to shut the trapdoor behind him. Enkidu didn't bother to climb. He jumped right over Ankaret's head.

'That's some cat,' she remarked.

'He is,' Henry agreed.

Mark and Ankaret ran ahead leaving Henry and Marigold to follow. When they reached Henry's bedroom, he paused at the open door. Should he stay in his room with Enkidu, even though his own stomach was rumbling?

Marigold guessed what was worrying him. 'It must be suppertime, Henry. You were asleep for ages up there in the attic. If you come down to the kitchen, you can get some food for your cat.'

How? Henry wondered. He carried Enkidu to the bed and, gently stroking his head, put him down and promised to bring him something good to eat. Though how he could keep his promise, he didn't know.

When Henry turned to go, Enkidu hadn't settled. He was sitting up and staring at Henry, his attitude tense and mistrustful.

'I'm sorry to leave you,' Henry whispered, 'but I'll be back soon.'

As he followed Marigold down the winding stairway, he couldn't stop himself from asking, 'Marigold, how are you going to get out of Timeless? The princess said that no one can, unless they come in on the equinox and leave within the hour. That's when I came in, and my aunt got out, but it's not like that now.'

She looked over her shoulder and smiled up at him.

'I'll get out. We just need moonlight, and the Shaidi.'

'But how?'

They had reached the dark passage leading to the kitchen. Marigold stood very still and, almost in a whisper, said, 'It's supposed to be a secret, but if it'll make you feel better, I'll tell you what Lucy told me. There's a coach made of autumn leaves and drawn by a very small pony, a forest pony. The Shaidi have laced the leaves together with forest magic, so that the coach can change its shape.'

'And will you be inside?'

Marigold nodded. 'I'll be wrapped in a gossamer dress and a shawl made of feathers.'

'Feathers?' Henry murmured.

'Thistle is the coachman,' Marigold went on. 'He is the grandfather and it was his idea. We'll fly over the Time Wall, over the great wall of trees, over the houses and hills and lakes. We'll settle in a tree and look like a raven, or rest among the weeds on a grassy bank, or we can bowl along a lane like an ordinary pile of leaves. In that way we can travel through the night without drawing attention to ourselves.'

It all sounded rather fanciful, and Henry wondered how much of it Marigold had made up.

'It will be the same for you when your turn comes. You'll stay there until the first rays of the sun show you the home you came from.'

Henry thought of Enkidu. Would he allow himself to be wrapped in a shawl made of feathers, or a jacket, perhaps, made of gossamer, which was probably nothing more than a large spider's web? Because he certainly wouldn't leave without Enkidu.

They approached the door into the kitchen. Henry heard voices and ran a hand through his hair.

'The green is fading,' Marigold assured him. 'The Shaidi's spells are mostly ephemeral.'

Henry took a deep breath and followed Marigold into the kitchen.

CHAPTER EIGHT
A Cry in the Night

The large room was buzzing with chatter. No one paid any attention to Henry at first. They were all too busy talking and serving themselves from large bowls of beans and greens. Two plates of nutty loaves sat in the centre of the table. Henry managed to take his place between Mark and Marigold without anyone mentioning his cat or his hair.

An old man sat beside Mrs Hardear. Henry hadn't seen him before. The man had long grey hair and a beard that overflowed on to the table, some of it lying on his plate. Henry felt someone should warn him about this, but decided it was not his place to do so.

A small glass of sparkling green juice had been placed beside Mark's plate. He pushed it towards Henry. 'Drink my juice,' Mark whispered. 'It'll make you grow.'

'Shouldn't I have my own?' asked Henry.

Ankaret made a face. 'It seems that you're not getting any.'

Twig had been walking carefully down the table, avoiding plates and bowls and pouring tea into empty cups. When she saw Henry, she gave a start and let the large brown teapot she was holding slip forwards. Hot tea spilt on to the table as she hissed, 'Cat-boy!'

The chatter subsided. Everyone looked at Henry. His cheeks burnt and he felt very cross. 'My cat's not here,' he protested.

'Bad boy,' Twig retorted.

Henry looked round the table, desperately searching for a glimmer of support.

From beneath thick eyebrows, he got a wink. 'Don't be foolish, Twig,' said the bearded man in a husky voice. 'There is no cat present. The boy is here to grow, so give him some juice.'

'Hear, hear, Professor!' Mrs Hardear gave Henry a wide smile and said, 'I'm Mrs Hardear, dear. We haven't been introduced due to that unfortunate poisoning. And this is Professor Pintail, who is a searcher. We are both guardians, of course.'

The old man nodded.

'By the way,' Mrs Hardear added, touching one of her huge ears. 'I am not hard of hearing.'

'I'm very glad to *hear* it,' said Henry, who could think of nothing better to say.

Beside him Marigold tried to suppress a giggle.

Twig, meanwhile, had righted her teapot and stood staring at Henry until, from the other end of the table, the princess called, 'Pull yourself together, Twig. Give Henry his juice.'

Twig swung round and stomped back up the table, where she put down the teapot, gave a little leap and disappeared from view.

Marigold's shoulders were shaking. 'Hear! Hear!' She giggled. The other children tried to hide their grins, but failed. Even the adults, at the other end of the table, were smiling.

Food was passed round. Everyone filled their plates. Henry found the nut loaves delicious. He was just putting a large forkful into his mouth when he saw Mark deliberately tip his glass over. For a second the pool of green juice fizzed, and then vanished, leaving the table completely dry. Mark immediately put the empty glass to his lips and pretended to drain it.

Henry blinked, not quite believing his eyes.

'It does that,' Mark whispered. 'I won't drink it.'

Henry gaped at the empty glass. 'What's the point of drinking it?' he said in a low voice. 'If it evaporates as soon as it leaves the glass?'

'It works if it's inside you,' Marigold told him. 'Look at me. I've grown two inches, so has Ankaret.'

'But Mark?' said Henry. 'Why doesn't he want to grow?'

'His mother died,' said Marigold in a low voice. She looked up the table at the adults. 'At first the princess tried to make him drink the juice, but then she sort of gave up. I think she's just hoping that if they keep offering Mark the juice, one day he'll change his mind and want to grow.'

'Our mothers are dead, but I still want to go home,' said Henry.

'Me too,' Marigold agreed. 'But Mark's first life ended only a few months ago, and he doesn't want to go back to the place where he used to see his mother every day.'

'But even if he grew he wouldn't have to go home,' said Henry.

'He would,' Marigold whispered. 'If the mayor ever caught sight of him, he'd be very suspicious. So they'll force Mark to drink the juice, one way or another.'

Mark suddenly got up from the table and left the room, muttering, 'No, no, no.'

'Now what?' said the princess. 'Has someone been asking about Mark's first life?'

'Cat-boy did,' said Twig, who had reappeared and was now walking daintily down the table towards Henry. She was holding a glass of green juice.

'I didn't.' Henry frowned at Twig.

'I believe you did.' Twig bent over and made a great show of placing the glass very carefully in front of Henry's plate.

Henry thanked her, rather reluctantly, and looked at the glass. He touched his hair and wondered what would happen next. Conversations began again. Marigold chatted to Lucy while Ankaret and Christian argued about food.

As Henry reached for the glass something dropped from the beam above him: a very small stone. It hit the rim of Henry's glass, sending it toppling over. The green juice formed a small puddle that frothed and sparkled and then vanished.

Henry noticed Twig glance quickly at the beam above him. Craning back his head, he looked up. There they were: four of them, sitting in a row: Mint and Marjoram and two other boys, smaller than Mint and wearing identical tobacco-coloured velvet suits. They looked a bit like large moles.

The two smaller boys began to argue. One had spiky hair, the other wore a hat like an acorn. Spiky-hair shoved Acorn-hat sideways, causing him to sway dangerously. With a loud squeak he grabbed his brother's arm and they both fell on to the table.

'Silly boys,' said Twig, pulling them to their feet.

'Really, Twig, we can't have this behaviour,' said

the princess. 'It is most unseemly. Can't you control your children?'

'They don't have a father,' Twig muttered, patting her sons' heads rather sharply. 'Say you're sorry,' she told them.

'Sorry,' said the boy with spiky hair. He bowed to Henry and added, 'Name's Nettle. Nut threw the pebble.'

'Didn't,' said Nut, making a face, but he turned to Henry, gave a small bow and said, 'Sorry, anyway.'

As Twig grabbed their collars and dragged them away, Nut whimpered, 'He shouldn't have brought a cat,' and he began to cry.

They both disappeared over the edge of the table.

Henry regarded the empty glass. He couldn't let the matter rest. He needed to grow. 'So can I have some more juice?' he asked.

'That's it for today,' said Twig. 'Juice doesn't grow on trees, you know?'

'Actually, I thought it did,' said Henry.

Twig turned her back and flounced to the end of the table.

An awkward silence followed. Henry thought he might have caused it. He felt very tired. Wearily, he got to his feet. He had no idea what he was going to say, but when he opened his mouth all the fear, the anger and astonishment that he'd felt when he lost his first life, began to pour out. And then he came to the day when he found Enkidu.

'In my second life I lived with my brother, who was very old by then, and my Auntie Pearl.' Henry looked round the table. He found he had everyone's attention. 'Our home was a little white house at the top of a cliff; the cliff was right above the sea.' He paused. 'It still is, I suppose, and it's still my home.' He could see it now, the house where he badly wanted to be, even though his brother who had been so very old when they met again, had died a year ago.

'One night,' Henry continued, 'I heard a cry, a wail, really, from outside. It was sad, loud and terrible; I could hear it even above the sound of the waves. It kind of reached out to me and I had to go to it. I put on my anorak and left the house. The sound came from way, way down the cliff, close to the sea. So I climbed down. It was very windy and the cliff was wet and slippery, but the moon showed me a tiny, dark thing on a ledge. It was a kitten; its crying sounded as frightened as I had felt when I lost my first life. I picked up the kitten and when I tucked it inside my anorak its terrible crying stopped.'

Twig had returned to the table. She stood watching Henry, but he couldn't tell what she was thinking. Everyone else was waiting for him to continue.

Henry took a breath and said, 'When I got back

to the top of the cliff my brother was angry that I'd put myself in such danger, and then I showed him the kitten and his face kind of changed. He told me that I'd saved a life, and so that life was my responsibility forever.

'And from then on, I felt that everything was all right. The kitten and I could begin our new lives together. My brother called the kitten Enkidu. He told me the name came from one of the oldest stories in the world.'

Henry looked at the faces round the table, but they had become a blur, and he wondered if his eyes were a bit teary. He wouldn't let tears fall. Instead he said fiercely, 'So you see Enkidu and I can never, ever be parted. We belong together.' And he marched out of the room.

The silence seemed to follow him, and his footsteps on the tower stairway echoed with loneliness. In a small recess halfway up the tower an oil-lamp shone feebly on the shadowy steps. A sound entered the stillness. Henry stopped. He heard a light rustle, a tiny patter, a faint breath. He was being followed.

'Do what you like,' Henry cried. 'I don't care any more.' He continued to plod up the steps. If he was still being followed his own heavy footsteps drowned out the sound. But when he reached his room he heard again that faint tap, tap of very small feet.

Henry went into his room and closed the door. An oil lamp had been placed on a chest of drawers beside the door. It cast a soft glow across the room.

Enkidu sat up expectantly. Food had been promised, but in his desperation to get away from the kitchen, Henry had forgotten.

'I'm sorry,' Enkidu.' Henry sat on the bed beside his friend and stroked his head. 'I'll go back later and get you something. No one's going to stop me, I promise.'

There came a light knock on the door.

'What do you want?' called Henry.

Whoever was outside his door either hadn't a voice, or didn't know what to say. A little villain, obviously.

It came again. Tap! Tap!

'Leave me alone,' cried Henry.

Several seconds passed. Perhaps they had decided to give up, Henry thought. He waited. There were no more taps, no knocking, no sounds at all.

'They've gone,' Henry told Enkidu.

Enkidu wasn't convinced. His ears twitched and he stared at the door.

Henry heard a rush of small, quavery mutterings. He strode to the door and flung it open. There, far below him was a little Shaidi, smaller than all the others – a girl in a deep purple dress, her hair fairer than her siblings' and slightly spiky.

'Who are you?' Henry demanded.

The tiny girl looked up at him. Her dark eyes were large and glistening, and her curling lashes very long. 'I'm Bramble,' she said.

'What do you want?' Henry asked roughly.

'To meet your cat?' It sounded like a question.

Henry scowled. 'What for? You want to torment him, I suppose, or put some nasty sort of spell on him. Well, you'd better change your mind, because Enkidu kills people.'

'Oh, I don't think so,' said Bramble, giving Henry a shy smile. 'Not after what you said. You made me believe I'd like to meet him.'

Henry took a step back. No matter how innocent she looked, he didn't trust her. 'Not a good idea.'

Bramble hung her head. 'I understand.' She darted a quick look into the room, clearly hoping for a glimpse of Enkidu. 'I won't insist.' She turned away with a small sigh.

Was that a purr coming from his cat? Henry could hardly believe it. 'Do you want to . . . to . . .?' he asked Enkidu.

The big cat jumped off the bed and padded across to the door. Brushing past Henry he came face to face with Bramble, or almost. He was taller by at least two inches.

'Oh!' Bramble's eyes grew even rounder. 'How handsome he is.'

Acknowledging the compliment, Enkidu gently rubbed his face against her shoulder. Bramble appeared to be holding her breath. With hesitant fingers she touched the long fur on Enkidu's head, and was rewarded with a deep purr. A little gasp escaped her. 'Is he growling?' She looked up at Henry.

'No, that's a purr. It means he's pleased.'

The tiny girl beamed. 'Of course, I remember now. A purr means happiness.'

'You'd better come in.' Henry stood back from the door and Bramble cautiously entered the room. Enkidu padded beside her. They made an odd couple and Henry had to smile.

When Enkidu sprang on to the bed, Bramble gave a little run towards it, almost tripping on her bootlaces. She tried again and bounced up beside Enkidu. Henry was impressed. He sat on the end of the bed, watching, a little anxiously, as Bramble became bolder, combing the deep fur on Enkidu's back with delicate fingers.

All at once, she said, 'Your life is ours now, Henry. We are responsible for you and we are bound to save you.'

'Oh, really!' Henry hadn't meant to sound so scornful.

'You don't believe me,' Bramble said sadly.

'How can I?' said Henry.

Bramble swung her feet. The untied laces slapped against her green boots. 'I can't tie my laces,' she murmured. 'My brothers tease me about it.'

'Do they?' Henry said, unhelpfully.

'They tease me a lot.' Bramble's feet came to rest, and she suddenly asked, 'What does Enkidu like to eat?'

Henry glanced sideways at her. 'Anything fishy, eggs and . . .' He paused, thinking of things that were not much smaller than Bramble. 'And stuff. I promised to bring him something tonight, but what with everything that happened, I forgot.'

Bramble slipped off the bed and made for the door. Before she reached it, Henry said, 'Wait, Bramble.' He couldn't watch those trailing, untied bootlaces without a pang of guilt. One trip and she might tumble headlong down the hard, winding stairs.

Bramble looked back and Henry got off the bed, knelt down and tied her laces.

'Thank you!' Her small voice was full of surprise.

'That's OK.' Henry was a bit embarrassed.

Bramble did a little skip, gave a giggle of delight and ran out of the room.

Henry found that he was feeling better. He seemed to have made a friend. '*You* have, too,' he told Enkidu. He lay on the bed beside his cat and closed his eyes, his former weariness returning.

Only minutes later, he was just drifting off to sleep when a small voice called his name.

Henry opened his eyes. Bramble stood in the doorway. She held up a tin, saying, 'For Enkidu. Sardines. There's a ring at the top so you can open them.' She put the tin on the floor, gave a little wave and was gone.

'Bramble!' Henry slid off the bed and ran to the door. 'Wait a minute.'

She was about to brave the steep stairway again, but glanced over her shoulder saying, 'I can't wait. I must help Marigold get ready for her journey.'

'Marigold!' Henry suddenly remembered that it was Marigold's last night in the house. 'I have to say goodbye to her.'

'You can't,' said Bramble. 'She is preparing herself. There are special garments and I am very good at fastenings.'

'When does she go?'

'When the moon is high and bright.'

'And if there are clouds across the moon?'

'We will sweep them away,' came the answer, as Bramble disappeared down the first step.

'But . . .' Henry began.

'I'm late,' she called, already far below him.

Henry picked up the tin of sardines and rolled back the top. 'You'll have to eat out of a tin,' he told Enkidu, placing the sardines on the floor beside the bed.

Enkidu had no objection. He was fond of his smart ceramic bowl at home, but he was aware that circumstances had changed, and sardines were a treat, however they were presented. He leapt off the bed and tore into the fish with relish.

Henry looked out at the night sky. He could see no moon. 'Not yet,' he murmured, and lay on his bed. Closing his eyes, he dozed a little and dreamt of the white house, the ocean and Charlie.

A thump on his feet woke Henry with a start. Enkidu had jumped on to the bed. Henry sat up. He remembered Marigold's journey and ran out on to the landing. If there was a moon, perhaps it was on the other side of the house. But how could he get to see it?

He began to descend the dim stairway. The next landing down was on the opposite side of the tower to his room. The only door here was small and worm-eaten, its rusty handle a large coiled ring. Henry tried it.

The ring turned and the old door creaked ajar. Shoving it with his shoulder, Henry managed to get it open wide enough to squeeze through. There was nothing in the room but a broken chair, illuminated by the light from the window. The light of the moon.

Henry went to the window. The glass panes were all missing and a blast of icy air made him shiver. Moonlight cast a silver glow across the garden.

And what a garden it was. Why had no one told him? Surrounded by trees, stone-flagged pathways wove their way between low-walled beds of herbs, shrubs and flowers. Untouched by frost, giant broad-leaved plants stood in tubs around a fountain. A stream sparkled its way about the plants and, in the distance, two night owls swooped and hovered above a meadow. Beyond the meadow lay the forest, dense and dark.

As his eyes became accustomed to the soft light, Henry saw small figures moving among the plants. 'Shaidi,' he murmured. He began to count them. There were at least ten, maybe twelve, all bobbing, reaching and snipping. A row of baskets on the central path were gradually filling with cut flowers and herbs.

Where was the coach? Henry screwed up is eyes, searching every corner, every shadowy recess, but there was no sign of a coach made of leaves or a tiny forest pony.

'I'm too late,' Henry told himself. But as he turned to go a terrible cry tore through the night, a tragic, melancholy howl. It made Henry's scalp tingle. The cry continued, on and on; it blew across the garden and through the paneless window of the room below, and when Henry ran from it, the sound pursued him. It drew faint echoes from the very walls. So many distant, sobbing voices.

'Who are you?' Henry cried, pressing his hands against his ears.

He reached his room and slammed the door against the tragic sounds, and in the quiet of his room a shocking thought occurred to him. *Had Marigold's journey failed?*

CHAPTER NINE
Ankaret and the Bomb

The gloom in the kitchen told Henry everything. When he arrived for breakfast, next morning, dejection hung over the table like an invisible cloud. Herbert and the princess were deep in conversation, and Henry caught a whiff of tragedy in their muted voices. Even the cockatoo, perched on the back of the princess's chair, looked depressed.

Mr Lazlo gave Henry a curt nod and Mrs Hardear smiled sadly at him, her head on one side. Miss Notamoth put a hand to her mouth as if she'd been surprised by a ghost. The professor hadn't appeared.

Henry took his seat beside Mark. Marigold's place had been laid, but her chair was empty.

'Did Marigold . . .?' Henry asked quietly.

Ankaret shook her head and tapped the table with her fingertips in a slow and solemn rhythm.

Lucy said, 'Poor Marigold. She wanted, so much, to go home.'

'What went wrong?' asked Henry.

'Someone was shooting night-birds,' Christian said gravely. 'The pony was terrified. It dropped into a tree and the coach was damaged, so they had to turn back. It would have been too dangerous to continue.'

Lucy sighed hugely, and the sound echoed round the room, just like the sobbing that had come from the walls the night before. Mark knocked over his glass of green juice.

Henry watched the precious juice fizz and evaporate. It seemed such a waste. He turned to Mark, saying, 'Marigold grew two inches.'

'And a lot of good that did,' muttered Ankaret.

'But we all have to grow,' said Henry. 'When I looked into that marble, I didn't know I would stop growing. After I disappeared my family probably thought I was dead. But I'm not. So it's like getting a second chance, a second life. And we must grow to . . . to take advantage of it.'

Ankaret and Christian stared at Henry in dismay. He had forgotten Mark.

'Don't talk about the dead,' cried the little boy, and he ran out, covering his ears.

From the end of the table the princess called, 'Did someone say the wrong thing again?'

'Cat-boy,' said Twig, placing a dish of something steamy before the princess. 'It's always Cat-boy.'

The saucepans above Henry tapped against each other in a ghostly breeze.

'Twig, give Henry his juice and let's have no more of this nonsense,' said the princess.

'Don't take any notice of Twig,' Christian advised, glancing up at the swinging saucepans. 'Or her children. They're still raw from their father's murder.'

'I didn't mean to upset Mark,' Henry said gloomily.

Twig came prancing down the table, holding a glass of green juice. She was about to put it beside Henry's bowl when he snatched it from her. Glaring up at the ceiling he said, 'You won't get it this time.'

Marjoram in her red skirt and green boots sat alone on the beam. Looking down at Henry with an earnest expression, she said, 'My brothers have promised to behave well.'

'We will, we will,' squeaked Nut and Nettle as they crawled out of a swaying copper cauldron. They swung themselves on to the beam, while Mint emerged from behind a tin bath that hung from a large meat hook. The three of them stood in a row and said, 'We promise!' Henry noticed that Bramble was not among them.

'You see, my children are good,' said Twig.

'I'm impressed,' said Henry.

But Twig suddenly put her leathery face close to Henry's and said, 'You saw it, didn't you? The beast with the torn face, the single eye, the scarred nose?'

Henry knew what she meant. 'Yes,' he said.

'My husband did that.' Twig leant so close Henry could smell her earthy breath. 'With his big, sparkly knife, my Moss did that, before he died.'

Henry swallowed. 'Did he?'

'He did,' Twig said triumphantly. 'And don't think you can charm my youngest child with your silly stories of kittens and cliffs.' From the corner of his eye Henry saw Mr Lazlo stand up. He walked towards them until he reached the empty space beside Ankaret. He was now directly behind Twig, who continued to scold Henry in a fast and furious little voice.

'She's very susceptible is my Bramble, and it's wicked of you to beguile her with lies. Kittens and cliffs indeed. All lies.'

'But they're not lies, 'said Henry.

'Wicked lies,' said Twig.

'TWIG, stop that!' roared Mr Lazlo.

Twig leapt. Henry reckoned she might have jumped right out of her boots if they hadn't been laced so tightly. She clutched her heart, turning on Mr Lazlo and panting, 'You shouldn't do that, Mr Lazlo! I could have died of fright.'

'I doubt it,' said Mr Lazlo. 'Twig, will you please leave Henry alone. It is bad enough having one poor child in distress, without you upsetting another.'

Twig flounced back up the table, leaving Henry in

peace for the time being. Henry cautiously sipped the green juice. It was sweet and yet bitter. He'd never tasted anything quite like it. The liquid tickled his tongue, but soothed his throat. Henry drained the glass.

When breakfast was over Henry took his bowl and spoon to the sink, where Christian had already begun to wash up. Lucy and Ankaret stood on either side of him, drying the wet dishes.

'Can I help?' Henry needed something to do.

Herbert tapped him on the shoulder. 'Princess wants to see you.'

'What for?' asked Henry, slightly anxious.

Herbert shrugged. 'She has her reasons. You'd better not keep her waiting.'

This sounded ominous. 'Where?' asked Henry.

'Library, of course.' Herbert walked away.

'Good luck!' Christian gave Henry a sympathetic grin. Lucy's smile was encouraging, but Ankaret said, 'Doubtless more trouble.'

'Why?' asked Henry.

Ankaret shrugged and walked out of the kitchen.

'Don't mind her,' said Christian, before adding, 'Ask the princess about Marigold if you get a chance. Everyone's very worried.'

'I bet Marigold is too.' Henry went in search of the library. It was two days since he and Marigold had visited the princess and he hoped that he could find the book-lined room again.

At the top of the main staircase, Henry stopped and listened. He stared down the long corridor at Marigold's door. Today the door was closed and no sound came from the room beyond. No singing and no crying. He turned away and, at length, came to the tall, shining doors with carved birds flying across the lintel. He knocked.

'Is that you, Henry?' The princess obviously reserved her soft voice for the library. Perhaps she was afraid of the dust, thought Henry.

'Yes, it's me.'

'Come in, then.'

When Henry opened the door he was once again assailed by scents of lavender and mothballs. A very tall ladder stood against the bookcase behind the princess, and a feather duster hung from the top. Twig had been at work.

'Come and sit down, Henry.' The princess patted a place beside her on the ottoman, and Henry cautiously obeyed.

'Don't look so concerned,' said the princess. 'I'm not going to scold you. I wanted to ask for your help.'

'Mine?' Henry was very surprised.

'I believe you are the very person, Henry. We have a problem. As you know, Ankaret and Mark refuse to go home. But they must, it is vital. Sooner or later they will be discovered here. We can't have this endless hiding and avoiding. One day the mayor and his henchmen might arrive unexpectedly. He believes that Christian and Lucy are my grandchildren. They were here before he began his Tuesday visits for treatment. But his suspicions would be aroused if he found Mark and Ankaret, and he would take them.'

'Why?' asked Henry, nervously.

'It's my belief that he has some association with the people on the outside who were after you, Henry.'

'But he can't. I mean these "outside people" can't communicate if Timeless is so . . . so cut off from the world.'

'Oh, they can, Henry. Every six months on the equinox, the mayor's deliveries arrive. Everything the town needs dropped inside, while the huge trucks race back to the world. Six months of news, papers, letters, documents and supplies. And in return, the mayor sends stolen gold and messages.'

Henry opened his mouth but not a sound came out.

'Lazlo suspects that someone may be spying on us.' the princess went on. 'People in the town have begun to infiltrate the forest, but only in the daytime, for now. The forest at night is a dangerous place.'

'Why doesn't Ankaret want to go home?' he asked. 'Why is she so moody and glum?'

'Ah!' The princess stood up and began to pace around the room, her rings sparkling in the early spring sunlight. A scatter of tiny sequins glinted on the sleeves of her long black dress and Henry had to stifle a sneeze.

'You've heard about the war, Henry?'

'My father died in the war, apparently,' he said. 'It was after I disappeared.'

'Not that one. There was another, twenty years later. It was worst in the city where Ankaret lived. She came from a happy home; loving parents and a new baby who she adored.' The princess stopped her pacing and stared out of a long window between the bookcases. 'And she was a pianist. Already at ten years old she had a huge talent. Her teachers thought she would become a concert pianist.'

'A pianist?' Henry was surprised.

'Indeed.' The princess began to speak as though she were describing a dream. '*One day Ankaret goes to see a friend, just a few doors down the road from where she lives. There is no warning of approaching aircraft, but while Ankaret and her friend are merrily eating jam and bread, they hear the siren and take shelter in the cellar. There is a bang, so loud Ankaret thinks her ears might fall off. And then a monstrous crashing, tumbling roar.*'

Henry held his breath. He could guess what was coming next, but dreaded to hear it.

The princess came and sat beside him. She gripped his hand, the rings on her long fingers digging into his flesh. '*Ankaret runs; runs and runs and runs towards her home. But there is no home. The bomb has blown it apart. It has gone. She sees a tangle of bricks and beams and burning rubble. Her family is buried beneath.*'

Henry stared at the princess's pale face. Ankaret's story was so much worse than his own, he could barely frame the question, but he had to know. 'How . . .?' he began.

Using both hands now, the princess clutched his fingers even tighter and he tried not wince as the hard stones bit into his palm.

'There was nothing left, but there, on the cracked pavement, lay a giant marble. It was as if the earth had vomited it up. That's how Ankaret put it. She stared at it, stepped closer and picked it up.'

'And looked into it,' said Henry.

The princess nodded slowly. '*In the sixty years that pass while Ankaret stands before her vanished home, bulldozers come, builders, roofers, plumbers and painters. When Ankaret sails out of the world in the glass sphere, she is looking at a bleak grey building. A home for difficult children. She stands there, in a daze, until someone takes her inside. No one believes her story. She is teased, bullied, ridiculed. All this she might have borne, if only there had been music, a piano. She is in despair when Treasure finds her.'*

'Treasure?' Henry sat up so sharply the princess dropped his hand.

'Yes, Treasure.' The princess smiled. 'You are related, I believe.'

'In a complicated way. But Treasure? You say she found Ankaret?'

'And rescued her,' said the princess. 'She is our best finder, Henry. We are the Guardians of the Lost.'

'That's sort of what Bramble said.' Moments passed while Henry tried to take all this in. Pearl's sister, Treasure, was a cook. She worked at Charlie's school. She was plump and rosy and always smiling. She was kind and funny and, once, when he had first been thrust through time, she had kept him safe. And now she was a Guardian of the Lost. Henry wondered if he was the reason. Had he begun it all?

'There were other lost children, Henry.' The princess grabbed his hand again. He wished she wouldn't. 'Goodness knows how many of those time-twisting marbles were created. We wanted to give you some time to adjust to your second life, and to grieve for the family you'd left behind. We thought you'd be safe so far from all the cities. How wrong we were.' The princess patted his hand and, to Henry's great relief, let it go.

113

'It was always our intention to help all the lost children to grow,' said the princess. 'But now there are people who are after you, we have no time to lose.'

'Couldn't you let Ankaret stay here?' Henry said. 'She could be hidden, surely, in this big house.'

'It is a problem.' The princess closed her eyes and pressed a fist to her forehead. 'I don't want to send her back to that dreadful place, but it is not only the danger from the mayor, Henry. Ankaret needs music, she needs a piano and we don't have one. In the whole of Timeless there isn't one. In fact, I'm not sure there are any musical instruments.'

Henry was shocked. 'None at all?'

'Not even an organ in the church,' the princess said sadly. 'And we cannot help her because,' she cleared her throat and continued awkwardly, 'we are not musical here, although we have many other talents. But without music Ankaret will wither. She will languish and fade away, I can see it already. Haven't you noticed the way she taps her knees, the table, every surface, her fingers always moving?'

Henry had noticed. He had thought it was impatience or anxiety. It had never occurred to him that Ankaret's fingers were pressing imaginary piano keys.

The princess had told Ankaret's story as though it were her own, and he wondered if the same thing had happened to her. Once again the princess had read his mind.

'In my case it was a kingdom that disappeared.' She sighed and gazed at the shadow of a cloud as it passed across the floor. 'It fell through the mountains; just like that, buried in snow. Only Lazlo and I survived. We had been out walking; it was such a lovely day.' She gave Henry a forced sort of smile. 'We became nomads, wanderers.' She reached for his hand again, but before she could touch him the door burst open and a ghostly, weeping figure appeared.

'Please!' cried the ghost, falling to its knees. 'I must try again. My family will be waiting.'

CHAPTER TEN
The Guardians

Henry recognised the voice, but not the creature sprawled on the carpet. Her golden hair had turned a dull silver, her hands were as pale as chalk and the strange garment she wore hung in torn strands, like broken cobwebs.

'Marigold?' said Henry.

She lifted an ashen face. 'I failed,' she said in a soft choked-up voice.

'You didn't fail,' said the princess. 'Some wretched game-keeper was shooting night-birds. The pony was frightened. It should never have happened. And it won't happen again, Mr Lazlo has seen to it. Now get up, girl,' the princess commanded.

The tattered girl slowly got to her feet. 'Please let me try again soon,' she pleaded.

'You must regain your strength,' said the princess, 'and that will take time. Look at your travelling robe. It's in need of some serious re-stitching as well.'

'I know I'm a sorry sight,' sobbed Marigold, 'but I don't feel too bad. I'll be all right tomorrow. I know I will. I want to see my family so much.' She began to weep copiously.

The princess appeared to relent. 'Child, come here.' She patted the empty space beside her. 'You can't expect to fly over the forest wall twice without feeling a little, how shall I put it . . .?'

'Almost dead,' sobbed Marigold.

'Un-dead,' Henry supplied, unhelpfully.

Marigold frowned at him. Drying her eyes on the corner of a ragged cobweb strand, she came and sat on the other side of the princess. The princess put an arm round her shoulders. 'You *will* reach your family again, dear girl. I promise you,' she said.

Marigold took a big, shuddering breath and said, 'Yes. Yes, I will. And Mr Lazlo has –'

'Seen to it,' the princess said firmly, but she obviously wasn't going to say how. Instead, she turned to Henry and said, 'I want you to hear Marigold's story. It will help you both.'

Henry glanced at Marigold, who was rubbing her tearstained face with a frayed sleeve. 'Why will it help?' he said.

'Because it's a wonderful story, Henry. Even better than yours.' The princess gave his arm an encouraging squeeze.

'Well?' he said, trying to sound casual. After all Marigold's first life interested him greatly, and so did her second life, come to that.

'Two hundred years,' Marigold gave a rueful chuckle. 'I am old, aren't I? My hair really should be this colour, and my hands withered and veiny. Actually, I should be dead.'

Henry couldn't see Marigold, on the other side of the princess, but he could tell that she was beginning to smile.

'I was playing hide and seek with my brother,' she said cheerfully, 'in my first life. My mother and father were not there much. We had a nanny and a governess, a cook and girls that cleaned and dusted and washed and made fires and carried heavy things. My life was better than theirs. I know that now and I'm sorry for it.'

'When did you lose it?' asked Henry.

'I went into the cellar. It was forbidden, but I went there anyway. I took a candle; couldn't see much for the dust and cobwebs, but there was an old chest, full of clothes. I pulled out a velvet jacket, black with gold braid along the hem, gold buttons and little pearls on the collar. It smelt of oranges. I whirled it round my shoulders and *chink* a marble bounced on to the stone floor.'

'Henry can guess what happened next,' said the

princess. 'But tell him how your second life began. Because that is extraordinarily marvellous – compared with some others.'

'Yes,' sighed Marigold.

Henry waited, expectantly.

'So when I came through that amazing other world in the marble, I was still in the cellar, but my candle had blown out and it was pitch dark. I screamed. And then – a miracle. All at once a light came on above my head. So very bright. The cellar was not as I had left it. The chest and the jacket had gone, the walls were white, and there were shelves of bottles and books, all neatly stacked. The steps up to the cellar door were clean and new. I began to climb them, frightened of what I might find, but curious too. The door at the top opened, suddenly, and two children looked down at me.' Marigold chuckled.

The princess dug Henry in the ribs. 'Listen,' she said.

Henry was listening, intently. He could have done without that jab, but the princess obviously wanted to make sure he didn't miss a word.

'They looked so mucky,' Marigold went on. 'I'd never seen a boy in jeans, and certainly not a girl. Their eyes went very round and their mouths opened, and the girl said, "It's *her*!" Just like that.'

'They knew who you *were*?' said Henry incredulously.

'They'd heard the story of the girl who disappeared two hundred years before,' said Marigold. 'They believed me. So did their parents. They welcomed me – joyfully. There were enquiries, of course, difficulties at the school and the doctor's and all that. But Mum and Dad got round it, somehow. They're artists and considered unconventional. Hooray for unconventionality, I say. They just accepted me.'

'Like Charlie and me.' Henry smiled. 'Didn't you find it hard to adjust? I know I did. But *two* hundred years . . .'

Marigold was silent and the princess said, 'Of course she did.'

'It took a while.' Marigold wrapped her hands round the torn gossamer in her lap. 'But they helped. They were so good. I'd been part of the family for a year when Treasure turned up, asking if there was a girl there who hadn't grown and who'd had another life.'

'Treasure again,' said Henry.

'She has her spies,' the princess told him. 'Thank goodness.'

Henry imagined a vast network of shadowy figures, spidering across the country – searching, listening, touching fingers and whispering. They would need a code if they used the internet, or even if they wrote to each other. No, he decided, if they were to evade the spies of whoever was out to get them, they would have to meet in out-of-the-way cafes, recognising each other by wearing a badge, or a brooch.

'A spider.' The princess touched a tiny silver brooch on her dress. 'Very small. A creature that creates a web.'

'Princess, you are always reading my mind,' Henry said accusingly.

'I merely follow a logical train of thought,' she said. 'I mentioned spies. Naturally, you tried to imagine how they operated.'

Marigold actually laughed. 'Treasure's spider is tiny. You would hardly notice it.'

'Amber with bars of gold,' the princess said fondly.

Marigold yawned and, glancing sideways, Henry noticed that her cloudy head of hair had fallen forwards and almost touched her knees. The princess told her to go and rest immediately. Mint and Marjoram would be sent to fetch the ruined travelling robes, and arrangements would be made for another attempt in the next few weeks.

'Weeks?' sighed Marigold, through another long yawn. She got up, with a moan, and trudged to the door.

As Henry followed, the princess called softly, 'Think about Ankaret, Henry. Think how you might help.'

Outside the library, Henry watched Marigold trudge along the corridor back to her room. He took the staircase, and when he reached the landing, darted a quick look in the mirror. His grass green hair was beginning to turn dark brown again. Henry grinned at his reflection and went down to the hall, where he stood and listened.

The cockatoo was telling herself a story in the kitchen, but the faint sound of voices came from the other side of the hall. Following the sound, Henry walked through a darkly furnished room of cabinets and leather chairs. The embers of a fire still glowed in the tiled fireplace. Henry reached a door. This led into a narrow passage where, directly opposite him, there was a blue door with 'BELLS, BOOKS and CANDLES' painted across the centre in shiny black copperplate.

Henry knocked on the door and a quavery woman's voice said, 'Who?'

'Henry,' said Henry.

'Not now dear,' said the voice. 'We're busy.'

'Miss Notamoth and I have important news to exchange.' This was definitely Professor Pintail's croaky voice. 'We'll see you later.'

'OK,' said Henry, puzzling at the professor's words.

As he walked back through the room of cabinets, Henry noticed a large window in the south-facing wall. He walked over to it. Just as he'd hoped, the window overlooked the back garden. 'I'd like to take a closer look at that garden,' he said, almost to himself.

'Better not.' Christian had come up behind him.

'But you can go out,' Henry complained.

'I've grown, so I'm not in danger, and the mayor believes I am part of the princess's family.'

Henry sighed. 'Do you know what they would do to us, if we were caught?'

'You won't be caught, Henry,' Christian assured him. 'You'll soon start growing, and then you can be off home.'

'But those people . . .?'

'Forget them.'

Henry nodded. 'OK. But the green juice will help me to grow?

'Gives you a kick start,' said Christian. 'Look at me. I've grown fourteen inches since I came here, and I don't need to drink the juice anymore. I'm thirteen now and growing the way I should.'

Henry smiled. Christian might have the face of a cherub, but he was the tallest thirteen-year-old Henry had ever known.

'Don't worry, Henry. You'll be safe with the Guardians.' Christian patted his shoulder. 'I'm off to play chess with Mr Lazlo.' He strode out, his big feet padding over the hall carpet until he reached a door that closed behind him with a creak and a clunk.

Hoping to find something for Enkidu to eat, Henry crept into the kitchen. A brown hen slept on a chair and the cockatoo sat alone on a beam. She put her head on one side and said, 'Bread in a bin, but stealing's a sin.'

'I'm not stealing,' said Henry. He had seen Herbert taking bread from a cupboard at the end of the room. Opening the cupboard door carefully he looked in. Bags of flour and sugar filled the top shelf, below them were tins, bottles and jars of pickled things. On the floor was a large bin. Henry lifted the lid. Inside were several crusty loaves and rolls.

'Uh-oh!' said the cockatoo.

'Shhh!' hissed Henry. Snatching a roll he rushed out of the kitchen and up to his room.

Enkidu had gone.

'Of course, he's gone out,' Henry said to himself. He imagined Enkidu leaping through a window on the ground floor and hunting in the long grass outside. But was it safe for him outside?

Ignoring the warnings, Henry rushed down the stairs and ran to the back door.

The door wasn't locked but heavy bolts secured it at the top and the bottom. Henry began to slide back the bolt at his feet. It made a loud grinding noise. He stopped and listened. No one appeared. He gave the bolt another tug and it slid back with a crack. He had to fetch a chair to open the top bolt, but that came easily.

Henry replaced the chair, opened the door, and was out. He gave a sigh of pleasure as sunlight warmed his upturned face. Closing the door softly, he ran round the corner of the house. Here a rough pathway led along the side of the house to a door set into a brick wall.

The door was fastened with an iron latch. Holding his breath in anticipation, Henry gently lifted the latch, pushed the door open – and almost jumped out of his skin.

'What have we here?'

Frowning up at Henry, from the other side of the door, was a very small man. A Shaidi, without a doubt. His large teeth were the colour of butter, his hair like a cloud of thistledown.

Henry could think of nothing else to say but, 'I'm Henry.'

CHAPTER ELEVEN
The Shaidi Workroom

'A rover!' The little man stroked his snowy beard. 'Here to grow. And have we grown?' He had a husky, rather gruff voice.

'Not yet,' said Henry. Clearly the little man hadn't connected him to the arrival of a cat.

'You will, you will,' said the Shaidi. 'Our juices have never failed.'

Henry realised that he couldn't possibly ask the little man if he had seen a cat. 'Could I – er – see the place where you make your – er – juices and stuff?' he asked.

The Shaidi frowned and scratched his ear. 'Well . . .'

'Please,' begged Henry. 'The girl called Ankaret has seen it, and she made it sound really wonderful.'

'Hm . . .' The old man hesitated.

'It's so boring inside,' Henry said disloyally. 'Nothing to do all day but wait to grow.'

The little man appeared to find this amusing. He gave

a chuckle and said, 'Why not? Why not? Follow me. I'm Thistle, by the way. My wife is Elm, my sisters Bee and Burdock, brothers Aspen and Comfrey. Aspen is at this very moment repairing the coach. The last journey did much damage.'

'Marigold's journey?'

'That's the one. Bad business. Pony very out of sorts, coach all askew. Someone taking a chance in the forest at night. Learnt his lesson, no doubt. And we'll try again. You'll know my daughter, Twig, I expect.'

'Um, yes.' Any minute now, thought Henry, Thistle is going to twig that I am Cat-boy. He felt guilty, not revealing himself, but hoped that he would see this wonderful workshop before Thistle guessed who he was.

'Better crawl, now,' said Thistle, pointing at the mossy paving between the flower beds.

The old man was no taller than the hedges that grew on either side of the paths. He couldn't be seen from the trees beyond the high brick walls that enclosed the garden.

Henry desperately looked around for Enkidu. There was no sign of him, so he obediently dropped to his knees and began to crawl after Thistle. The old man's pace increased every second. In no time Henry's knees were so sore he longed to stand up, but even when they came to the meadow, Thistle made him keep below the level of the grass. And here even the Shaidi himself hunched down beneath the feathery tips of wild plants.

They reached the trees at last and Thistle declared it safe enough for Henry to stand. He got to his feet and rubbed his aching knees.

'It's as well to be out of sight, Rover Henry,' said Thistle, shaking grass seeds from his hair. 'The less those townspeople know the better.'

'Has no one ever guessed that you're here?'

'My good beard, no,' said Thistle. 'They believe we are all gone and, sadly, most of us are. Our grandchildren will be the last little folk in the world, as far as we know.' He squared his shoulders and set off down a narrow path through the trees.

Henry followed, wishing that he could prove the little man wrong.

Thistle began to sing in a light, whispery voice. Henry couldn't make out every word, but he soon realised that Thistle was telling him how, for thousands of years, the little folk, the Shaidi, had existed, close to the earth and hidden in the trees; how things that grew in the earth listened to them, and were happy to support them.

As Thistle sang Henry was astonished to find himself walking through the seasons. Snowflakes floated before him, touching his head and shoulders, and then raindrops came pattering through the trees, now frost sharpened the air and dead leaves sparkled in his path. After the frost the sun climbed higher; shadows danced between the trees and hidden creatures scratched and rustled in the undergrowth.

'Am I growing older?' Henry murmured.

'We are all growing older, Rover Henry,' Thistle chuckled. 'But some of us are not growing taller. If we were seen that would be the end of us. Our friendship with the earth is called magic, that's why they tried to get rid of us. Magic makes us different, they said, and different is dangerous.'

Henry became aware of a distant hammering, a whirring, a humming and a tapping. He saw no barn or workshop ahead of him. And then Thistle said something that brought him to a standstill.

'Luckily for us,' said Thistle, 'the princess and her friends are all witches.'

'*All of them?*' Henry exclaimed, turning towards the ancient house. 'You mean everyone in there is a *witch?*'

'Everyone,' Thistle affirmed. 'Except for the children.'

Perhaps Henry shouldn't have been so surprised. After all there was magic in his own family. But *all* of them? 'Even Herbert?' he asked.

The little man gave a high-pitched titter. 'Yes, even

Herbert. Most of them hunted down, tormented and banished. We have an understanding with people like that. The forest welcomes them. Of course, the cockatoo was once . . .' He searched for a word, but unable to find one, said, 'Something else.'

Henry remembered stories of princes turning into frogs, girls into birds and boys into hares. 'I never knew . . . I never dreamt . . .'

'No need to worry about it,' said Thistle. 'They are all reformed now.'

'Oh,' said Henry, for want of a better word. He stepped slowly after the old man, while the hammering, tapping, whirring and humming got louder and louder. They came to a very small door – just a door, no walls around it – a slim mossy green door standing in the middle of the path with trees crowding densely on either side. Thistle opened the door, walked through and beckoned to Henry.

He hesitated, remembering Shaidi tricks.

'Come, Rover Henry.' Thistle waggled his forefinger. 'There's nothing to fear.'

Wasn't there? *Too late now,* thought Henry, *I'm already halfway there*. He bent down and stepped into the workshop.

It turned out to be a vast circle of trees, growing so closely together there wasn't a glimmer of light between them. Within the circle five elderly Shaidi were busy working at separate tree stumps with surfaces as smooth and shining as any table.

The little people were all humming contentedly as they worked. They were dressed in velvety shades of green and brown, the colour of their hair ranged from white to dove grey, their ears were longer and sharper than Twig's, and their noses redder. One had a short grey beard, another a long white one.

Two of the female Shaidi turned the wheels of miniature sewing machines, while softly sparkling gossamer slipped beneath their needles. White-beard hammered at a tiny broken wheel, Grey-beard stirred the syrupy contents of an iron bowl. The fifth Shaidi, a rotund auntie-looking person in a purple apron, sniffed different coloured liquids in glass jugs, before pouring them into bottles.

'So here we are,' said Thistle. 'My wife, Elm, and sister Bee are mending Marigold's travelling robes; my brother Aspen repairs a coach wheel, while my sister Burdock and brother Comfrey are . . . how shall I put it?'

Burdock looked up from her sniffing and said cheerfully, 'Cooking up spells, brother, that's what we are doing.'

'And this is Henry, a new rover,' Thistle announced, closing the door.

Henry waited for cries of outrage and horror. But none came.

The little people looked up briefly, nodded and smiled at Henry before returning to their work. He saw that shafts of sunlight beamed directly on to each worktop, and any number of bottles, large and small, twinkled on the planed surfaces of fallen trees around the edge of the circle.

'What if it rains?' Henry asked Thistle.

'But we are inside,' said Thistle, throwing out his arms and indicating the gently swaying treetops.

'Inside?' Henry was puzzled.

'Yes, inside,' Thistle repeated and, without lifting their eyes from their work, the others all repeated, 'Yes, inside!'

'I see,' Henry said politely.

He was just admiring the tiny tools hanging from low branches at the back of the room – if it could be called a room – when the door opened and, to his dismay, Twig appeared.

'YOU!' she cried, pointing up at him. 'Who let you in?'

'I did, my dear, said Thistle. 'Our new rover wanted to see the workroom.'

'NO!' she screamed. 'This is Cat-boy. The boy that brought the cat to kill us all.'

'Cat-boy?' came a chorus of elderly voices. 'CAT-BOY?'

'GO!' screeched Twig.

Henry fled through the door. As soon as he was out a shower of hailstones rained down on him. He ran, blindly, trying to shield his head and face with his hands, while hailstones, as big as marbles bit into his fingers and battered his shoulders. He hoped Enkidu was sheltering somewhere safe.

'Ouch! Ouch!' cried Henry as he stumbled through the forest. Twice he lost the path and crashed into a tree, but, at last, he reached the meadow, and began to crawl through it. Now it was his back that got the beating.

They're using some nasty sort of magic to punish me, thought Henry. Once he was in the garden, however, the hail stopped, and it was only his knees that suffered on the hard paving.

With a huge sigh of relief Henry crawled round the side of the house and got to his feet. Carefully opening the old, mildewed door, he slipped through and closed it firmly behind him.

Someone had bolted the back door again. Henry rattled the handle and pushed it with an aching shoulder, but it wouldn't budge. There was nothing for it but to try the front door, but that was locked and bolted as well.

'At least there's a door knocker,' Henry said to himself as he lifted a heavy iron badger-head and rapped on the thick, scarred wood.

He remembered the spies, and decided not to call out. Perhaps, even now, someone was watching, or listening. He found that he was shivering and lifted the badger-head again.

BANG! BANG!

No one came. Henry sat down and clasped his knees. The paving stones were cold, his back was cold, and his fingers were freezing. He hummed to stop his teeth from chattering. *I'm not going to get anywhere doing this*, he thought, *I'm just going to die of cold.*

Henry got to his feet again, grabbed the badger-head – and fell headlong into the hall as someone opened the door.

'Stars above!' Herbert exclaimed, staring down at Henry. 'Have you been in the ring with an elephant?'

'What?' croaked Henry, getting to his knees. Standing seemed impossible.

'You've got a bump the size of an egg on your forehead.' Herbert helped Henry to his feet. 'Where have you been, Rover Henry?'

'W-workshop,' stammered Henry. 'They found out that I was Cat-boy.'

'You've been told never to go out,' Herbert said severely.

'I was looking for Enkidu. He's disappeared,' groaned Henry.

'No, he hasn't,' said Herbert. 'I saw him only five minutes ago, creeping up the back stairs.'

'Oh, Enkidu!' cried Henry, in relief and exasperation. 'Where was he?'

'Cats like to have secrets.' The porter put an arm round Henry's shoulders and took him into the kitchen. 'Hailstones,' he said, looking at the bump again, 'if I'm not mistaken.'

Henry nodded. He couldn't stop shivering.

'The Shaidi don't mean to hurt,' said Herbert, 'it just happens when they're frightened. Now, how about some hot soup,' he suggested, seating Henry in front of the stove. 'Happen to have some chestnut soup on the boil.' He stirred a pan of thick liquid, bubbling on the stove. 'Do you like chestnuts, Henry?'

Henry gave another shivering nod.

'Here we are, then.' Herbert ladled some of the golden liquid into a bowl and placed it on the table before Henry.

Henry put both hands round the bowl and gave a sigh of pleasure. The heat warmed him right through, from the back of his neck to the tips of his toes. The broth was a warm nut-brown, its surface shimmering like sunshine. Henry lifted the bowl to his lips – and then put it down. He stared at the topaz-coloured

135

windowpanes, at all the copper pans and bowls, ladles, forks, colanders and cleavers shining above him. They swung in a breeze that he couldn't feel, and a soft, musical sound echoed about them.

'What is it, Henry?' The porter drew out a chair and sat beside him.

'No-nothing,' Henry said weakly.

'Drink up, then.'

Henry looked at the twinkling soup. 'It's – erm, too hot.'

The porter regarded him with his curious yellow eyes. 'It's not just that, is it, Henry?'

Henry hesitated. 'No,' he admitted. 'It sounds a bit – well – silly. Well, not silly exactly, because some of my relatives are, well, unusual to say the least, but . . . but . . .'

The porter leant closer. 'Yes? Spit it out!'

'Well,' said Henry. 'Thistle, well, he said that . . .' Henry swallowed, '. . . you were all witches.'

Herbert threw back his head and guffawed loudly. 'You don't think I'm trying to turn you into a frog, do you?'

'Could you?' asked Henry. 'If you wanted to?'

The porter laughed so loudly he could obviously be heard from many rooms away, because, one by one, Miss Notamoth, Mrs Hardear and Professor Pintail, all appeared through different doors.

'Herbert, I haven't heard you laugh like that for years,' said Professor Pintail. 'What's the joke?'

Miss Notamoth and Mrs Hardear hovered round the table, glancing anxiously at each other.

'Our covers are blown,' Herbert told them. 'Young Henry here *knows of our past.*'

Miss Notamoth gasped, Mrs Hardear flung her hand over her mouth and the professor, after looking keenly at Henry, pulled out a chair and sat down opposite him.

'Now you mustn't worry, my boy,' said the professor, sweeping the end of his impressive beard off the table. 'We have renounced all that, haven't we, ladies?'

'Oh, absolutely,' said Miss Notamoth.

'We don't even dabble,' added Mrs Hardear, pulling on a large ear.

'Not for years,' said Miss Notamoth, flapping her sleeves.

'We promised the princess, when we came,' said Mrs Hardear. 'That was the deal. No more spells, no sorcery, no magic. It's all finished.'

'But why?' asked Henry. 'I mean, what's wrong with the odd spell, a nice one, of course. My own relatives, for instance, can be very helpful.'

The four ex-witches, two of whom could more properly be described as wizards, stared at Henry in silence. He got the impression that they might, secretly, agree with him.

Henry gazed at the nutty soup. He was cold and hungry, and the witches were not, so to speak, active. They watched him take a sip and smiled when he gave an 'mmm' of pleasure and licked his lips. The chestnut soup really was delicious.

'So why did the princess forbid magic?' Henry asked his audience.

'She lost her kingdom because of it,' the professor told him. 'The princess comes from a family of great power, great magic. Trouble was, there were too many witches in the family. If you have twenty witches all trying to outdo each other, what do you get?'

Henry waited for the answer.

'An avalanche, Henry,' said Mrs Hardear. 'That's what you get. By great good fortune the princess was out walking in the mountains with her little boy. They were the only ones in the kingdom to survive.'

'As for the kingdom,' the professor added gravely, 'it was gone: the castle, the town and all the surrounding villages. Every inhabitant – all gone, buried under a mountain of rock and snow.'

'And all because witches were showing off.' Behind her large, round lenses, Miss Notamoth's magnified eyes gazed tragically at Henry.

'Oh dear!' It sounded a bit lame but Henry couldn't

immediately think of anything better. He took a sip of the delicious soup and was about to take another when Lucy ran in from the hall.

'Mark's gone,' Lucy cried urgently. 'Ankaret saw him go through the back door and climb the front gate. She climbed after him, and went a little way into the forest. But she lost him. If someone outside catches him . . .'

'Then it'll be the end of him,' said Herbert dramatically.

CHAPTER TWELVE
Talk of Goblins

The princess was told.

She came to the kitchen with the cockatoo on her arm and sat at the head of the table, while the bird perched on the back of her chair. Everyone was there, even Twig, though her children were absent, mercifully in Henry's opinion.

'Who saw Markendaya go?' asked the princess.

Ankaret said, 'I did.'

'How did he get out so quickly? He must have stopped to unbolt the door.' The princess looked accusingly around the room.

Henry had to own up. 'I – er – unbolted it,' he said.

'You!' The princess glared at him.

'I wanted to go out,' Henry said defiantly.

'But you haven't *grown*.' The princess banged her ringed fingers on the table. 'You haven't even begun to grow, and until you do, you must not go out. You know this, Henry Yewbeam, do you not?'

'Yes,' said Henry, through his teeth. 'I just wanted to see the garden, and get a bit of fresh air.' He didn't like to mention his cat. 'It's quite normal for someone to want fresh air, especially if they live by the sea.'

Everyone looked rather surprised and Mr Lazlo said, 'You are too curious for your own good, Henry Yewbeam, but I suppose that is why you are here. Inquisitive children gaze into marbles.'

Miss Notamoth began to titter, Mrs Hardear made a snorting noise and the professor gave a short guffaw. The princess smiled, in spite of herself. Somehow Mr Lazlo had broken the ice. Henry didn't find it funny, but he supposed that ex-witches occasionally needed some light relief.

It didn't last, however, because Herbert suddenly remembered that the back door had been bolted when he passed it, not more than ten minutes ago. 'And you came in by the front door, Rover Henry,' he said, scratching his head.

'The back door wouldn't open,' said Henry.

'So who . . . ?' began Mr Lazlo, searching the faces of the assembled children and ex-witches.

After several offended denials and a long silence, Ankaret mumbled, 'I did.'

'You, Ankaret?' said the princess. 'Do you mean to tell me that you let a small boy leave the house and then bolted the back door against him?'

Ankaret tapped the table with her long, pale fingers. 'I couldn't stop Mark,' she said. 'I called and called, and then I thought the mayor might come in that way, and take us all by surprise.'

'Why would he run away?' said Christian. 'He knows he's safe here.'

'I think he was afraid that he'd be forced to drink the juice,' Marigold said thoughtfully, 'and then he'd be sent home, whether he wanted to go, or not.' She glanced at Ankaret, who looked away.

Everyone agreed that Mark had to be found as soon as possible. Mr Lazlo harnessed his black stallion and rode off into the forest. Herbert followed in a green trap, drawn by a small chestnut pony. The three ex-witches sat in the back.

From an upstairs window, those left behind watched the small expedition depart. In spite of feeling a bit guilty, curiosity got the better of Henry and he made the mistake of asking if the people in the trap ever used broomsticks. The princess gave him a severe look and didn't reply.

'Does the chestnut pony pull the coach?' asked Henry, hoping this question would get an answer.

'If you're asking about your journey out of here,' the princess said coolly, 'then no. The forest pony is much, much smaller than the chestnut, and a better size for the Shaidi.'

'But . . .' Henry began. He could get no further. After all, what did the size of a pony matter, when Mark was lost and in danger?

Two hours passed. The princess and the children had lunch and Henry was allowed to drink his green juice in peace. On the beam above him, Twig's children ate their meal in silence. Even they were aware that Mark's disappearance could be dangerous for all of them.

Henry wondered why Bramble wasn't eating with them, and then he saw her, perched on a far rafter, her untied laces flapping against her small swinging feet. He wondered if her brothers had been teasing her again.

The day wore on but the search party didn't return. When supper was over Henry managed to get his piece of bread up to Enkidu, but after chewing it politely for a while, the big cat looked regretfully at Henry, and pushed it away with his paw.

'I'm sorry, it's not your sort of stuff, is it, Enkidu?'

Enkidu gazed steadily at Henry.

'Where do you go in the daytime?' Henry asked. 'Do you find an open window, or catch mice somewhere in the tower?'

Enkidu gave nothing away, but his sorrowful expression told Henry that his cat was still hungry. Henry thought that Herbert might give him an egg, if he pleaded with him. And then he remembered that Herbert was still out and Twig was in charge of the larder. He'd never get past her. But surely she would eventually go to bed.

Henry lay down and waited. He dozed for a while, but was woken by urgent voices outside. He got up and crept halfway down the winding stairs. The search party had returned. They were all in the kitchen, their voices rising and falling: the professor's high croak, Miss Notamoth's buzz and Mrs Hardear's harsh grunt.

Henry crept to the bottom of the stairs, tiptoed across the passage and stood as close to the kitchen door as he dared. They were giving the princess an account of their search. It seemed that Mark had not been found.

'We were waylaid by goblins,' said Mrs Hardear. 'They're utterly unreliable.'

Henry thought he had misheard, but no, for Mr Lazlo added, 'Goblins. Useless creatures. I could get no sense out of them.'

'Wilful,' said Miss Notamoth. 'Teasing us with silly jokes, said they'd seen a boy talking to foxgloves. Foxgloves, indeed.'

'Couldn't describe the boy, of course,' said Professor Pintail. 'Goblins have a different sense of shape to us. Small is big, big is small, foxgloves could be people wearing purple.'

'I do hope that poor boy hasn't come to any harm,' said the princess.

'I doubt it,' said Mr Lazlo. 'Goblins are nothing more than tricksters.'

'The wolves aren't so bad if you speak nicely to them,' said Miss Notamoth.

'Lynx are a different kettle of fish,' grunted Herbert.

'But not at all fishy,' said the professor.

'It would be so much easier,' Miss Notamoth said a little diffidently, ' if we could use our skills.'

There were several loud coughs and clearing of throats and Miss Notamoth said quietly, 'No, of course not. Just a silly thought.'

Goblins? Wolves? Lynx? Henry tiptoed back across the passage and began to creep up the squeaking stairway. He heard Mr Lazlo's deep voice propose they have a few hours' rest and continue the search at dawn, then the shuffle and patter of feet leaving the kitchen, and calls of, 'Sleep tight, don't let the slippers bite.'

The Guardians had an odd way of saying good night, thought Henry. He decided to stay in his room until he was quite sure everyone else was asleep. He sat on his bed, stroking Enkidu's soft head and thinking about Mark, alone, among the lynx, the wolves and the goblins. He thought of the professor's words. 'Foxgloves could be people wearing purple.'

He remembered that Peter and Penny Reed wore purple sweaters.

Henry jumped to his feet. 'They've got him!' he said aloud. 'Taken him to Number Five! I'm sure of it.'

Henry felt responsible. He had drawn back the bolts. He had left Mark with an easy escape. There was no question. It was up to him to rescue Mark. 'Who's afraid of goblins?' He gave a nervous laugh.

Enkidu wasn't fooled. He knew a false laugh when he heard one. His miaow was long and concerned.

'Who's afraid of wolves?' Henry said, loud and almost cheerful. 'Who's afraid of lynx?'

Enkidu gave a low, rumbling growl.

'OK, just a bit afraid,' Henry admitted. 'But if I don't go tonight, it will be too late. They'll hand Mark over to the henchmen, and who knows what will happen to him then?'

Enkidu jumped off the bed.

It would be good to have the big cat's company. Henry went to the cupboard and found a red anorak. It was two sizes too big for him, but it would have to do. He had just zipped himself into the anorak, when there was a light tap on the door.

'Who is it?' Henry said cautiously.

'Bramble,' came the tiny voice. 'With food for Enkidu.'

Henry opened the door.

When she saw the anorak, Bramble looked anxious. 'You are going somewhere, Henry?'

'I am,' Henry agreed. 'And so is Enkidu. But he would very much like a meal before we go.'

Bramble walked in, holding out a tin of sardines. 'Henry,' she said. 'It is the hour of midnight. Where are you going?'

Henry told her.

'Into the forest? You cannot.'

'Mark has been kidnapped,' said Henry, 'and I think I know who took him. Everyone else is exhausted and asleep. I have to go and rescue him.'

'Then I have to come with you,' Bramble said firmly.

'No, no,' Henry exclaimed. 'Excuse me for saying so but you are too small, and I heard the . . . well, the Guardians say there were goblins and wolves and lynx in the forest. I'm sure it's all nonsense, but –'

'It is *not* nonsense, Henry.' Bramble stamped her small foot, laces flapping. 'There are worse than goblins in the forest at midnight.' She opened the tin of sardines and set it before Enkidu.

'Worse?' Henry said, uneasily.

'Much worse,' said Bramble, watching Enkidu gobble down the fish. 'Mighty things, hungry things, treacherous things.'

'Oh,' Henry sat down heavily on the bed.

'But we will go, Henry,' Bramble said gravely, 'because Mark must be saved and no one must know about this house and what happens here. No harm will come to you if I am beside you, because I am of the forest, just as *they* are, and they respect us.' She gave a small giggle. 'Also, little villains have tricks up their sleeves.'

Henry got to his feet again. 'You are not villains, Bramble,' he said.

'No we are not,' she said, 'but it's the name we were given, and sometimes it suits us very well.' She turned to the door. 'Meet me by the back door in a few minutes.'

'Wait!' Henry quickly knelt and tied her bootlaces. Bramble beamed, and was gone.

Henry let Enkidu swallow the last fish and wash before they descended the stairs. Bramble was waiting by the door when they stepped into the passage. She carried a small lantern in one hand, and a rush broom in the other. Her tiny face peeped up at him from layers of leafy garlands, so many, in fact, that the rest of her could hardly be seen. There were red and purple berries among the leaves, and they gave off a warm, peppery smell.

'Take a garland, Henry,' she said, 'and one for Enkidu. They will keep you safe.'

Henry bent down and lifted two garlands over

Bramble's head. It was surprising how well they fitted themselves around Henry's neck, and also his cat's. They were, after all, very different sizes. Enkidu looked disapproving at first, but he didn't shake the plants off.

'Open the door, Henry,' said Bramble.

He saw that the bolts had been drawn back.

'I can do locks and bolts,' Bramble explained, 'but I haven't learnt handles yet.'

Henry opened the door without asking questions, nor did he ask any when the big iron gates swung open at their approach. He took care to close them behind him, though.

The trees reached out to them, drawing them closer. And then they were in the forest. But it was not a place that Henry recognised. The forest had changed.

CHAPTER THIRTEEN
The Night Forest

Henry found that he was breathing a different kind of air: ancient, filled with tastes and scents he'd never known. And there were sounds, light at first, but deepening as they moved further into the forest.

Bramble swung her tiny lantern and giant trees loomed into view. They groaned and muttered, and Bramble returned the mutters, swinging her lantern faster. The beams climbed into the night, making the highest branches glitter like stars.

They plunged deeper, along a track that was now a thin gleam, like the wake of a snail.

'Why is the forest so changed from how it is in the day?' Henry whispered. He dared not speak loudly.

'It is as it was,' Bramble replied, 'when Shaidi first arrived. And we have kept it this way.'

'But when I came, it was not like this,' said Henry.

'It only reveals itself at night.'

This explanation would have to do, Henry thought,

but Bramble went on, 'Our grandfather says it has to be this way. If the forest betrayed its age in daylight, it would call attention to itself. In the dark, mysteries are to be expected.'

'True,' Henry agreed.

As the dense air pressed about them, Henry felt a light tap on his head, and then another. The third tap was considerably heavier. 'Ouch!' Henry whirled round, but could see nothing. 'Something hit me.'

'Tricks,' Bramble said calmly. She swung her lantern out in front of her and there, caught in the light, was a blue person, about twice the height of a Shaidi.

'Ha! It's the smallest one,' said the blue person. His nose was wide and flat, his nostrils huge and hairy. He had no lips at all and his eyes goggled out of his face like shiny puff-balls. His yellow hair was very sparse, his ears large and pointed. He wore a short tunic made of fur.

'Yes, it's me,' said Bramble fearlessly. 'We are looking for a boy, my friend and I.' She turned to Henry. 'This is a goblin, Henry.'

The goblin hissed, revealing a mouth full of crooked blue teeth. 'Boys not allowed,' he snarled. 'Not after dark. Gwoblins don't like. Gwo away.'

Enkidu suddenly sprang into the light, growling at the goblin.

151

'Ahhh!' shrieked the blue man, stepping back. 'Gwoblins not like cats. Bad smallest Shaidi for bringing it! Gwo back!'

'We've come this far, and we're not going back,' said Bramble.

Henry was becoming impatient. He wasn't quite sure what the goblin might do, but he felt inexplicably safe within his magic garland. 'We're in a hurry, Mr . . . er . . . Goblin,' he said. 'Have you seen a boy, bigger than you, but smaller than me? We think he came into the forest today.'

'Shan't tell.' The goblin glared at Enkidu.

'Well, did you see a foxglove?' Henry asked, rather desperately.

'Might have.' The goblin scratched a hairy knee with his long nails. His fingers appeared to have four joints instead of three, and Henry counted seven toes at the end of each fishy-looking foot.

'There's no time for silly games,' Bramble said sharply. 'We must find the boy before daybreak.'

'Oooo, silly gwames, is it?' the goblin cackled. 'I'm not telling you nothing.' He turned away, but before he could take another step, Bramble had pulled off one of the garlands and flung it at the goblin's head.

'Oooow! Eeee!' shrieked the goblin, pulling at the leaves. The garland had slipped down his head and was now stuck fast on his large pointed ears. 'It hurts, smallest one! Gwet it off! Gwet it off!'

'Tell us about the boy,' Bramble demanded.

'I did see it. Ooo! Ooo! Ow! Hair like coal. Ow! Ow!' He tugged at the leaves. 'I followed close to edge of forest. Brave me, don't like edge of forest. Too bright. Ow! It spoke to the foxgwoves. Two of them. Ow! Ow! They grabbed, pulled, took it away. Take it OFF, smallest one!'

Bramble swung her lantern. She sang something that sounded like, 'Grishago, ogershoo,' and the garland flew off the goblin's head, landing at her feet.

'You are cruel,' said the goblin, rubbing his ear, which had turned a bright shade of purple. 'Better not go further. There's a gwoul on the path tonight. Not nice.'

'We'll take our chances, thank you,' said Henry, wondering what a gwoul was.

'You'll be sorry!' The goblin hopped off the track and could be heard chuckling away to himself as he disappeared into the trees.

'What is a gwoul?' Henry asked Bramble.

'He means ghoul, and it eats dead people,' said Bramble, picking up the goblin's garland and putting it round her neck. 'But we are not dead, so it will leave us alone.'

Henry hoped she was right.

They pressed on. A lynx crossed their path. It glared

at the small party, bared its teeth and hissed. Henry shrank back, keeping Enkidu behind him. Once again Bramble sang in a strange lilting language. The lynx hunched down, growling, but it wouldn't move off the track.

'We'll have to go round it,' Bramble whispered. She moved off the path, swinging her lantern, and walked past the lynx. Henry followed with Enkidu on his far side, but the lynx could smell another cat and leapt up, snarling.

Bramble waved her lantern in the lynx's face. Momentarily blinded by the bright light, it crept away, complaining dangerously.

Miss Notamoth was right about wolves. Three of them trotted past the little group without a sound.

They came to a line of mossy boulders and scrambled over them, arriving on earthern slabs, veined and knobbly. And then a row of massive trees blocked their path. There seemed to be no way round them. Bramble swung her lantern and the light moved across the great naked columns. Very slowly two of the trees shifted apart, and the three adventurers dashed through.

'That was weird,' said Henry. 'They were almost human.'

'Giants,' said Bramble.

'What?' Henry thought of the boulders. 'Giants' toes? I never thought giants were *that* big.'

'Too big to see us,' said Bramble, 'and their eyesight is bad. But they felt my lantern light and knew we were there. They're friendly in their way.'

Henry was glad to hear this.

They continued down the narrow, faintly glowing path, and it seemed to Henry that the trees pressed closer the further they walked. He began to wonder if they would find any town at all at the end of their journey. Behind the closely packed trees things moved, some lumbering, some rushing and jumping, others sliding and slithering. Above them pale winged creatures swooped and floated. Were they birds? It was hard to know.

They heard the ghoul before they saw her, wailing and groaning. Enkidu growled, and out she rushed across their path. For a moment she stood there, staring at them with hollow black eyes, her mouth a gaping hole rimmed with blood, her grey sleeves stained with crimson patches.

Bramble swung her lantern and specks of fire blew into the ghoul's face. With a shriek of pain she leapt into the air and soared into the trees, still screaming.

Henry's heart beat wildly. He knelt and hugged his cat, while Bramble sang into the night, 'Grishago, ogershoo!' repeating the strange words over and over until the screaming stopped.

For a moment the forest was silent, and utterly still,

and then the night creatures began to move again.

'Is it far now, Bramble?' Henry asked, ashamed to find himself still on his knees.

'Not at all,' Bramble said cheerfully.

It was hard to believe, but she was right. Once Henry was on his feet again it took them only a few minutes to arrive at the edge of the forest, and then they were on the path behind the houses in Ruby Drive.

The heavy, ancient air had lifted, and the sounds of the past had gone. All at once, Henry realised that the world they had reached was even more dangerous than the forest behind them. Little villains were supposed to be dead and gone, and he was a wanted boy who hadn't begun to grow.

They found the back garden of Number Five. Henry looked down at Bramble. 'Stay out of sight,' he whispered. 'You are not safe here, Bramble.'

She smiled up at him and slipped behind the wall.

Henry unlatched the gate and began to move down the path. He hadn't made plans. He had no idea how he would find Mark and get him out. But he wasn't going back without him.

There was a movement behind the long windows into the garden. In the thin gleam of moonlight, Henry saw a small face. It was Mark. Henry was about to leap forwards when two hands came from behind the boy in the window, and grabbed him by the shoulders.

CHAPTER FOURTEEN
The Goydrok

Henry froze. He hadn't imagined this. His instinct was to run to Mark, but he knew it would be hopeless. If he was seen, they would both be prisoners.

But what would become of Mark now, and if he had told his captors about the Shaidi and the Littles' house, what then?

'So what,' Henry said to himself. As he took a step towards the window, a startling shower of sparks hit the glass pane, making it glow like fire. There was a scream and a roar, and Henry saw the door fly off its hinges and soar into the air.

For an instant a tall man and a boy could be seen bathed in brilliant light, but just as suddenly they vanished in a cloud of fog. The grey cloud thickened. It filled the garden and Henry almost choked on it. He began to shuffle backwards and had just reached the open gate when something ran into him, hitting him in the stomach.

'Who is it? Who is it?' cried Mark.

'Shh!' breathed Henry. 'You're safe. Come quickly!'

He took Mark's hand and they began to run. Ahead of them a tiny light bounced and swung.

'Henry, it's you!' Mark whispered. 'You found me!'

'We did,' said Henry softly. 'Bramble helped. That's her, ahead of us, with Enkidu, my cat.'

'Your cat,' Mark whispered. 'But . . .'

'She's not afraid of him.'

They caught up with the bobbing light and Henry saw that Bramble was taking little, leaping strides that lifted her above the ground for several paces, before she bounced back to earth again.

'The forest is close,' she said in a small, breathy voice.

Henry could see nothing but a thin path of light thrown out by Bramble's lantern. But he knew when they were in the trees because he could smell the strong, earthy scents and feel the pressure of the air from long ago.

'Safe now,' said Bramble.

They might have been safe, but Henry kept running, dragging Mark along with him until the small boy croaked, 'I can't run any more. My legs hurt, my arm hurts and I'm so, so tired.' He pulled his hand away from Henry's and sank to the ground.

'We must keep going,' hissed Henry. 'Come on!

Come on!'

'Let him rest,' said Bramble. 'No one will dare to enter the forest at this hour.'

'I'm sorry.' Henry knelt beside Mark. 'That Mr Reed gives me the creeps. I just wanted to get as far away as possible.'

'Me too,' mumbled Mark.

Henry looked over to the little Shaidi, standing patiently beside Enkidu. 'The flying door and the fog, that was you, Bramble, wasn't it?'

'It was this,' she said, waving her little rush broom. Then she took off one of her garlands and slipped it over Mark's head. 'To keep you safe,' she said.

Mark gingerly touched the leaves. 'Thanks,' he murmured.

'I did my first handle, didn't I?' she said. Her voice had become very faint.

'Not exactly,' said Henry. 'I'd call it more of a hinge job.'

'But I did the handle first.' She sounded disappointed, as if turning a handle was more impressive than causing a door to fly off its hinges.

'Of course you did,' Henry said kindly. He turned to the boy breathing heavily beside him. 'Mark, why were you at the window? Were you trying to get out?'

'They were horrible people, although they pretended to be nice at first. I said I didn't want to go with them,

159

so they started to pull and push me.' Mark took a deep breath. 'When they thought I'd gone to bed, I listened at the kitchen door and I heard them say they'd hand me over in the morning. I remembered what happened to you, Henry, and I decided to try to escape while they were all asleep, but that awful man must have heard me.'

'We were just in time.' Henry got to his feet. 'Can you go on now, Mark?'

'S'pose so.' With a long sigh, Mark slowly stood and grabbed Henry's arm. 'But how will we find our way home?'

'Look! There's a line at our feet,' said Henry. 'See it shining? It leads all the way to the Littles' house.'

'I see it!' said Mark in surprise. 'How does it glow like that?'

Bramble stepped in front of him. She swung her lantern up and down, up and down as high as it would go, and the shining path snaked forwards through the trees, as far as they could see.

'Your lantern,' Mark said in awe.

'My lantern.' Bramble's words came out almost like a sigh.

'But the forest is so big.' Mark stared at the never-ending pathway.

'So we'd better get going.' Henry linked his arm through Mark's and they followed Bramble down

160

the track, with Enkidu pacing carefully beside her. And while they walked Henry warned Mark of the dangers they had to expect, because the forest at night was old and fierce, and home to creatures thought to be long gone.

'But Bramble can keep us safe,' Henry told Mark, 'with her garlands, and her lantern and her broom.'

'Can she?' Mark sounded doubtful, in spite of all that the tiny girl had done, he was still afraid. 'I didn't tell those people,' he said, 'when they asked where I lived. I didn't tell. I said I'd been left at Martha's Cafe, just like you, Henry. I said I'd decided to go exploring and got lost. So they don't know about us being at the house, and they don't know about the Shaidi.'

'Good,' said Henry. 'Well done.'

Although Mark had been warned to expect danger, he wasn't prepared for the ghouls. There were three of them this time. Screeching and clawing, their gaping mouths rimmed red, their black sightless eyes huge in their chalk white faces. Bramble swung her lantern, but its light was weaker, and her magical words were so faint they sounded little more than the whispering of leaves.

Henry felt a claw dig into his ankle, another tore at his arm and a foul-smelling liquid streamed down his face. *A ghoul's saliva,* he thought. With his free hand he lashed out at the spongy, floating creatures, while

161

Mark clung to his other arm, screaming for help.

The flame in Bramble's lantern grew dimmer, and her words had now ceased altogether. As the lantern light faded, the shining pathway slowly vanished, until it was nothing but a thin glimmer at their feet.

Henry could hear Enkidu hissing and growling, he could hear the ghouls cursing the big cat as he bit into their soft bodies, and clawed their bony hands, but Bramble's lantern had all but gone out and Henry was afraid that nothing could save them now.

Clinging to each other, the boys sank to the ground, and the heavy, shapeless ghouls settled on top of them, suffocating, stifling, crushing the life out of them.

And then they'll eat us, thought Henry.

'Are we going to die?' Mark wheezed into Henry's ear.

He didn't dare to answer. In fact, he thought he had taken his last breath when light suddenly burst over them, and a clear little voice sang out, 'Grishago, ogashoo! Grishago, ogershoo.'

The ghouls rolled off the boys. They stood, unsteady in the light that had now become so bright Henry could barely look at it.

'Grishago, ogershoo!' sang the little voice. 'Grishago, ogershoo!'

The ghouls screamed. They flapped their wide white arms, their mouths stretched across their masklike faces, their eyes now a glowing white.

On and on went the little voice, chanting into the night until, with trembling hands, the ghouls hid their eyes and drifted off the track. Henry watched them disappear into the trees, their dreadful wailing echoing through the forest and waking all the creatures that preferred to sleep at night.

As soon as the ghouls had gone, the brightness faded until it was a mere spark flickering beside Henry's feet. By its fragile light Henry could see a tiny, crumpled figure. He knelt and touched Bramble's curly head.

'Bramble, you saved our lives,' said Henry. 'But I think the effort was too great.'

For a moment she didn't speak, and then a frail voice said, 'I am not bright inside, Henry. I am . . . I am . . . falling.'

'She's dying,' cried Mark. 'Her light has gone out. My legs are crushed and we'll never get home.'

'We will,' said Henry firmly. 'I'll carry you both if I have to.' He pulled Mark to his feet, but the small boy slumped against him, clinging to his arm.

I've been in worse situations, Henry told himself, remembering his hateful cousin Ezekiel's torments. For a moment, he felt defeated. Worse than injured Mark, was Bramble's small, motionless body.

Enkidu suddenly brushed against Henry's legs. In

the dim, forest light he saw the big cat lower his head and nudge the tiny girl. A weak sigh escaped her, and then Enkidu did something unexpected. He turned his back on Bramble, pushed her with his back legs and sat down.

Henry was puzzled. Enkidu must have a purpose; he never did anything without a reason. Suddenly, Henry understood. 'He wants to carry you,' he exclaimed. 'Bramble, can you hear me? Enkidu is offering to carry you.'

'That would be good,' breathed the little girl.

'Let me go, Mark.' Henry unfastened Mark's clinging hand and sat him on the grass. Bending over Bramble he gently lifted her up and laid her on Enkidu's back, her head resting between his ears.

'Lantern,' she whispered.

Henry held the lantern next to her small hand, and her fingers closed tightly around the handle. Immediately, the flame grew. 'I feel Enkidu's heartbeat,' she said, smiling.

Henry picked up the little broom and slipped it into his pocket. 'It's a piggy-back for you,' he said, hoisting Mark on to his back.

The track began to glow again and they continued on their way. In spite of the grunts and roars of nameless creatures, Henry felt more hopeful with every step. Running was out of the question, but the lantern light, small as it was, kept them safe.

All was well until the Goydrok came. When the earth gave a shudder and the trees muttered uneasily, Henry thought a storm might be on it way. But the shuddering became a rumble, and footsteps, like the muffled thud of falling rocks, came thundering behind them.

'Run, Henry,' cried Bramble. 'Run. It's the Goydrok.'

'Goydrok? What's that?' said Henry.

'Run, run, it's the worst. I had forgotten the Goydrok. I can't stop it.' And with that Bramble's light went out, and the shining pathway vanished.

'Bramble!' cried Henry.

'My light has gone but I'm still bright,' she whispered. 'I can feel Enkidu's beating heart. Run, Henry. You must escape its reach.'

Henry didn't think he could, with Mark slumped on his back, but urging himself forwards he began a limping sort of jog. He couldn't see where he was going, but he could sense Enkidu moving beside him, finding the way, somehow. And then the wind came, hitting them in the back and knocking Henry off his feet. Mark tumbled to the ground and Henry rolled beside him.

'What's happening?' croaked Mark.

'Don't know,' Henry groped desperately for Enkidu and Bramble.

The thunderous footsteps drew closer, but Henry found that he couldn't move. It was as if a thousand arrows pinned him to the earth. Painfully he turned his head and saw it, or rather saw its glowing outline; a gigantic mound with eyes like fiery coals. Its dreadful breath swept towards them, choking, burning and sickly.

'Bramble?' Henry muttered hopefully.

There was no reply.

Henry grabbed Mark's hand, screwed his eyes tight shut, and waited.

And waited.

Thunder growled about them, but behind it Henry thought he could hear the steady rhythm of hoof-beats. The wind that howled above them seemed, if anything to strengthen, it became a whirlwind, a hurricane. Pushing his free hand through the blast, Henry found Enkidu at last and, wriggling closer, he flung an arm over Bramble and the big cat.

It's as if two currents of air are fighting over us, thought Henry as the wind tugged their hair, first one way and then another. But suddenly a different sound rose above the scream of the wind. It was as if the forest had a language of its own, a voice that spoke like the bleat and bellow of animals, like rushing water, falling leaves, rattling pebbles and the songs of night-birds.

Lifting his head as far as he could, Henry saw a great horse several paces in front of him. A beast conjured out of the darkness. Henry quickly shut his eyes and pressed his face into the earth. There was a deafening howl behind him, the ground heaved and groaned, and terror shook the very trees.

When the terror had fled, the silence was so profound, Henry wondered if he was still breathing. Daring to raise his head again, he found that he was bathed in moonlight. The great horse stood before him, blacker than the night, its thick mane glistening. The bearded rider leaned towards Henry and spoke.

'I see that you have found our runaway,' said Mr Lazlo.

CHAPTER FIFTEEN
Miss Notamoth's Surprise

Henry remembered little of what happened after Mr Lazlo found them. Strong hands lifted him on to the stallion and there he sat, with Mark clasped before him, and Mr Lazlo at his back.

'Bramble?' he had mumbled.

And the little voice, clear as a bell, sang out, 'I have Enkidu to carry me.'

When Henry woke up in the morning, sunlight was streaming into his room, Enkidu breathed steadily at his feet, and he felt ravenously hungry. Hoping he wouldn't be too late for breakfast, he threw on his clothes and, promising to bring his cat something to eat, he ran down the tower steps.

He paused at the kitchen door, suddenly wondering if he had done the right thing in rescuing Mark.

It seemed that he had. When he walked in, the faces turned towards him were all smiling. Marigold, looking much recovered, even clapped her hands.

Henry walked to his seat amid a chorus of, 'Incredible', 'Well done, boy', 'We'd never have thought it.' There were also murmurs of, 'Terrible risk', 'Never to be attempted again,' and 'Thank your lucky stars Mr Lazlo found you.' But, by and large, everyone was in favour of Henry's midnight escapade. Professor Pintail had not yet arrived, but then he was often late for meals.

Henry took his place between Mark and Marigold, who patted him heartily on the back.

'It was Bramble, really,' said Henry. 'I couldn't have got through the forest without her.'

Everyone nodded, and the princess said, 'She is, indeed, a brave, brave girl.'

'Is she . . . is she OK?' he asked.

'Her family will make sure of it,' said the princess.

Henry glanced up the table and saw that Mr Lazlo was eating his breakfast in an unconcerned way.

'And Mr Lazlo, of course,' said Henry. 'We probably wouldn't be here at all if . . . if . . . So thank you, Mr Lazlo.'

Mr Lazlo raised a hand and nodded.

'Congratulations all round, I'd say,' said Herbert.

There were murmurs of agreement and approval before everyone went back to their toast and porridge.

You can never please all of the people all of the

time, and someone was not going to let Henry's daring rescue alter their opinion of him, no, not one jot.

Twig walked daintily down the table and, placing Henry's glass of juice before him, stood with her hands on her hips, looking at him resentfully.

'Thank you, Twig,' said Henry, ignoring her stare.

'Don't thank me,' she retorted. 'I'm under orders. I'd give you a good hiding if I had my way. You took my youngest child into grave danger. She nearly died. How could you do such a thing? It's a disgrace.'

Feeling guilty but needing to defend himself, Henry leant over his plate, and said, 'And I think it's a disgrace that you haven't taught your youngest child how to tie her bootlaces. She could easily trip on them, fall and hurt herself really badly. I think you're a very lazy mother.'

Several loud gasps rippled round the vast kitchen.

Twig, too shaken to speak, compressed her leathery lips, walked unsteadily up the table and jumped to the floor.

'Congratulations!' said the cockatoo.

'You were a bit hard on Twig,' Marigold whispered.

'But it's all true,' said Henry.

'You seem to have made quite a friend of Bramble,' said Christian. 'We hardly see her.'

'It's Enkidu,' Henry admitted. 'She loves him.'

'LOVES?' Christian exclaimed, and the other children stared at Henry in amazement.

'She's very brave,' said Henry.

'Very,' Mark agreed, tipping up his glass of green juice. Once again the spilt juice fizzed and vanished.

Henry picked up his own glass and drank the sweet-smelling bitter-tasting liquid.

Across the table sharp nails beat a rhythm on the wood. Henry put down his glass and looked at Ankaret. She stared back with eyes that held no hope; her face was paler than ever, her red hair unbrushed and wild. The princess had told Henry that he, perhaps, might help Ankaret. But how, when the only life she could return to was so bad? And then he thought of the piano.

Henry picked up his spoon and put it down again. The beginning of an idea stirred in his mind. Perhaps second lives could be changed. He picked up his spoon and ate his porridge with enthusiasm.

Mrs Hardear approached Henry after breakfast. 'Come to my room,' she said, 'you and Mark. You are unaware of it, but you both look in need of some patching and painting.'

'Do we?' Henry touched his face in the places Mrs Hardear was regarding with such interest. 'I haven't got a mirror,' he said.

'No need for alarm,' said Mrs Hardear. 'I'll see you

in my room in five minutes.' She might have been on an unwieldy broomstick, the way she zoomed and swayed up the main staircase.

'Mrs Hardear, I don't know how to find your room,' Henry called. But the ex-witch appeared to be hard of hearing today.

Luckily Mark knew where to find her. As they made their way along the shadowy corridors, the whispering voices followed them. Henry wondered if he was the only one to hear them. They didn't seem to affect Mark at all. In fact, he began to talk about his first life, about how happy he had been until his mother got sick. She had wanted to go back home to India, but she was too ill and his father hadn't been able to help her.

'Your father probably didn't know how to help her,' Henry interrupted, 'not like a doctor would.'

Mark scowled at the floor. 'He didn't try hard enough. She went into hospital, but I didn't want to see her, all pale and sleepy, with plastic curtains and machines and cords circling round her like aliens. So I stayed outside her room when my father went in. Then I ran from there, down many stairways and long corridors, until I came to a place full of boxes, and as I stood there, wondering where to go next, a big marble rolled close to my foot.'

'So you picked it up and looked into it.'

'It was very wonderful. So beautiful. I thought I might stay inside it forever, but suddenly I was out in the world again. I was in the same room, but the boxes had moved. I found my way up into the hospital and a woman came towards me, all in dark blue, with a face like a bad stone. When she saw the marble, she kind of grabbed it. I told her my mother's name, and she said, "She's not with us any more. Come with me." She took me out of the hospital and along a busy street. Her grip was so hard I wanted to cry out.'

Henry found that they had stopped moving. They were in a particularly dark corridor, the wallpaper patterned with large green flowers. 'And then?' he asked.

'A woman all in red passed us. She had a good face and a tiny spider on her collar. It made me want to touch it, and all of a sudden, I was calling out to her, "Help me! Help me, please." She turned and looked at me. She smiled and said to Stone-face, "Where are you taking that child?" "None of your business," said Stone-face. "On the contrary," said Spider-on-collar.

'When she said that, I pulled my hand away, and ran to her. "Keep running," she said, and we both ran. She held my hand and we zig-zagged through the crowds.'

They started to move again, and now that Mark had begun his story, he seemed to enjoy telling Henry how the woman with the spider on her collar had taken him to someone called Treasure, who worked as a cook in a school like a castle.

'She's my aunt.' Henry came to a halt again. 'Well, we're related anyhow.'

'Related?' Mark said with a touch of admiration. 'They were Guardians of the Lost, Treasure told me. She said I'd been gone for three months, that it was in the papers, and she said that because of the marble, I might never grow again, so I must come here, to the Littles' house, and they would help me.' Mark hung his head, half-closed his eyes and muttered, 'I didn't tell her my mum wasn't with us anymore, because that means you're dead.'

Henry wondered if 'Not being with us' really meant that someone was dead. Perhaps Mark had got it all wrong.

Before Henry could question Mark, they had walked through a whispering bead curtain and into a large sunlit room. It was walled with shelves of twinkling bottles. Mrs Hardear sat in a rocking chair, surrounded by piles of bright cushions. She had changed into a long black dress patterned with red and white triangles, and a black shawl, which might have been expected of a witch, Henry thought.

'There you are,' said Mrs Hardear. 'Take a cushion, both of you.'

Henry chose a pile of red cushions, Mark a pile of blue and green. Mrs Hardear examined their hands, pinched their arms and legs, peered into their hair and, grasping their chins, turned their heads to left and right.

'Hm,' she said. 'No permanent damage, but let's get those scratches seen to. Did anything touch you in the forest? Other than plants, of course.'

Henry and Mark exchanged glances, and Henry said, 'Ghouls,' then added, 'and a goblin.'

'Goblins are ineffectual,' said Mrs Hardear. 'Ghouls are a different matter. You will need an antidote.' Up she got and scanned her shelves, touching bottles, picking some up, peering into them and replacing them. After scratching her large ears for some time, she suddenly said, 'Ah!' and withdrew a large bottle of sinister-looking deep mauve liquid.

Henry and Mark looked at each other, grimacing, while, from a green cupboard, Mrs Hardear pulled out a wad of soft grey stuff. 'Spiderwebs,' she said, nodding at a tank of flies the boys had failed to notice.

'What . . .?' Henry began uncertainly.

'Keeps the spiders happy,' the ex-witch explained with a cheerful smile. She poured some of the mauve liquid onto the wad and approached Mark, who shrank back. 'Don't be silly,' said Mrs Hardear, grabbing his hand and dabbing it all over. Then she rolled up his sleeves and wiped his arms, removed his socks and shoes and dabbed his ankles, rolled up his trousers and wiped his legs. Mark had given up by the time she came to his face, sitting patiently, while she rubbed his ears.

Henry watched Mark's face turn from a light brown to a rather streaky mauve, and then he allowed Mrs Hardear to repeat the process with his own face, legs and arms. She was working on his badly clawed ankle when he asked, 'Is Bramble going to be all right?'

'Of course,' said Mrs Hardear. 'She's in her mother's care.' She paused in her dabbing, and looked up into Henry's eyes. Her own were an alarming mix of pink and green. 'Twig is an excellent mother,' she said solemnly. 'You were quite wrong there, Henry.'

'But Bramble's laces . . .' Henry argued.

'Twig gave that responsibility to Nut and Nettle. The older children were taught always to instruct their younger siblings in washing, dressing, tying, reading and writing. Everything, in fact, that a young person should be able to do.'

Henry was mortified. 'I didn't know,' he said.

'Obviously not,' said Mrs Hardear, arching an eyebrow. 'Nut and Nettle are not bad boys, but they like to tease their little sister, and sometimes they can be unkind.'

'*I* shall teach Bramble,' Henry said firmly.

'I believe that, thanks to you, Henry, Bramble is having instruction in tying, right now,' said Mrs Hardear. 'The Shaidi prefer to take care of their own.'

Henry felt thoroughly put in his place. He pulled on his socks and, glancing at Mark, he said shyly, 'There's something I'd like to know about the house.'

'Yes?' Mrs Hardear pulled an ear.

'Perhaps it's just me, but I can hear voices, whispering. Sometimes they laugh, sometimes they are sad.'

'Yes, dear. There are whispers,' said Mrs Hardear. 'You get used to them. In fact,' she put her head on one side, 'voices from the past can be very comforting.'

'I see,' said Henry. He would have liked to know more, but Mrs Hardear had begun to make shooing motions with her slightly stained fingers.

'Off you go now,' she said. 'You'll be right as rain.'

So the boys said their 'thank you's and left the bright room, the mystery of the whispering still unsolved.

As soon as they stepped into the corridor, they were astonished to see Miss Notamoth approaching, very fast. She was, in fact, almost flying.

'Markendaya! Markendaya!' She cried. 'Oh, Mark, dear. I have something to tell you.'

Mark stared at her, almost in horror, 'What?'

'Your mother is alive, dear!' Miss Notamoth's eyes were even rounder than usual, her thick lashes quivering.

Mark stared at her in disbelief. 'How do you know?' he whispered.

'Professor Pintail has only just this moment returned. We had our suspicions, but she'd been back to India, you see, and left no trace. However, now she is here again and dear Treasure found her.' Miss Notamoth's very thin fingers folded themselves into her wide sleeves, and she shook them delightedly.

'She's alive!' cried Mark, his eyes shining. 'I want to go home soon, soon.'

'And so you shall. I told Twig to give you both double-strength juice. Now, run along. And Henry, get something for your cat to eat, I'm sure he could do with it.'

How did she guess? Why did she care? But another questioned burned on Henry's tongue. 'How did the professor . . .?

'Don't ask, dear,' said Miss Notamoth. 'It's just something that happens to us when we wish it. Nothing to do with spells, I assure you.' She gave them a wide smile and waving her lacy sleeves, floated away down the corridor.

Henry was very surprised when Herbert gave him two hard-boiled eggs and the remains of a kipper.

'This doesn't mean that you're forgiven for bringing a cat into the house, Rover Henry,' said Herbert, 'but you deserve a favour for rescuing young Mark.'

'Thank you.' Henry took the plate of cat treats.

'I'm going home,' Mark sang out.

'Yes, I believe that's on the cards,' said Herbert airily. 'If you drink your juice.'

'I will, I will,' Mark said fervently.

'I hope Mrs Hardear knows what she's doing,' Herbert remarked as Henry and Mark left the kitchen.

The boys stopped in the doorway. 'What d'you mean?' asked Henry uneasily.

'Nothing, nothing,' Herbert cheerfully replied. 'Mauve is such an alarming colour, that's all. For the skin, I mean.'

The boys touched their faces, and Henry said, 'Do you . . . sometimes . . . disagree with each other about . . . about . . .?' He didn't like to mention witch's treatments or magic potions.

'All the time,' Herbert said unhelpfully. 'But the princess won't let us make an issue of it.'

Henry found himself saying, 'Or *BANG*, and we'd all sink beneath the earth.'

'Exactly,' said Herbert, and then laughed, which relieved the boys no end.

Enkidu was pleased with his breakfast. When he had finished he sat on Henry's bed, cleaning his thick black fur and snow white paws.

Cross-legged on the floor, Mark watched, his large, dark eyes thoughtful and admiring. 'I'd like a cat,' he said.

'Perhaps, when you go home, your mum and dad will get one for you,' said Henry.

Mark turned to him with a wide smile and said, 'Yes. Mum likes cats. But I won't need one now, will I?'

There was a knock on the door and, without waiting for an answer, Marigold opened it and poked her head in. 'My, you two look like aliens,' she exclaimed.

When Mark and Henry grinned, she added, 'Did you know your teeth have gone purple?'

The boys clamped their lips together and Henry grunted, 'Come in, why don't you?'

Marigold swung round the door and danced in, followed by an anxious-looking Ankaret. They sat on the second bed and Marigold said, 'Mark, we heard about your mum.'

'I'm going home,' he cried, clasping his face in his hands. 'I'm going home.'

'When you've grown,' Ankaret remarked.

'Yes, yes,' Mark said, 'and I will.'

Marigold asked if the boys felt all right, with their mauve faces. This made Henry feel a bit queasy, but Mark said that being painted was a lot better than being kidnapped. So Henry just said he'd felt a lot worse.

'Witch's stuff always wears off,' said Ankaret knowledgably, 'unless they want it to be permanent.'

'You knew they were all witches?' Henry said accusingly.

'Thistle told me, but I didn't want to scare you lot, so I kept it to myself.' Ankaret gave what could have been a smile.

'*All of them?*' Marigold looked shocked. 'They're *all* witches?'

Mark said, 'Even Herbert?'

'Even Herbert,' said Ankaret. 'Lucy and Christian know, but they've been here much longer.'

For a moment Marigold looked dumbfounded, then she said brightly, 'I suppose they can make the Shaidi's magic even more potent, and my next journey will succeed. I know it will. Perhaps in two weeks' time, I'll be going home.'

'And I will, too!' Mark declared. 'Just as soon as I start growing.'

Henry looked at Ankaret, who gave him a challenging stare. 'I'm not going anywhere,' she said.

Henry hesitated before he made his suggestion. 'I've been thinking,' he said. 'When I go back, that is if I begin to grow, you could come with me.'

Ankaret gave him another hard stare. 'Don't be ridiculous,' she said scathingly. 'They can't take two at once.'

Henry wasn't going to give up that easily. 'But if they could?'

'It's impossible!' she almost shouted.

'No!' cried Henry, throwing out his arms. 'This house is full of magic, if only the witches were allowed to use it. Why can't the coach carry two? Why can't a horse, however small, pull a coach for two?'

'You haven't seen it,' said Marigold. 'You have to shrink inside robes of caterpillar silk. You stop breathing, you can't see, hear, feel . . . you're as tiny as an ant, or it seems like that.'

'That's all right, then,' said Henry. 'Two ants don't weigh much more than one.'

When Ankaret laughed at this, Henry added, casually, 'And we've got a piano.'

He could see that he had made an impression. Ankaret became very still, her eyes widened and she stretched her fingers across her knees, lifting each one, carefully, as though she were trying to remember the notes of a tune.

'And now you must tell us what happened in the forest,' said Marigold.

'And why your faces are mauve,' said Ankaret, her voice quiet and unsteady.

When Mark and Henry had finished the long account of their extraordinary journey – the attack of the ghouls and the Goydrok, Bramble's bravery and

Enkidu's resolute support – they came to Mr Lazlo's appearance, and then the call to lunch could be heard, even from their high tower room.

They ran down to the kitchen, all four, in their own way, feeling somehow more hopeful, even happier.

The next two days passed quickly. Mark drank his double strength juice and his fingernails began to grow. The mauve paint faded and his skin acquired a healthy glow. Henry lost his mauve face but nothing else happened. He was told that, in his case, growth wouldn't show for a while, as his second life had lasted so long. Ankaret watched him, with interest.

Every night when Henry climbed up to his lonely tower room, he would think of Pearl and Charlie, and the home he longed to see again, and a little stab of fear would make him wonder if the Shaidi's potion would ever work for him. It was then, when he was at his most despondent, that the soft whispering voices would take on an unexpectedly cheerful note, almost as though they were willing him to take heart.

'I don't know who you are,' he would murmur. 'But thank you. I *will* grow,' and his words would be followed by a long whispering sigh of contentment.

Life was progressing at a steady pace, by and large, until the day of the pan-shining, and then everything changed.

CHAPTER SIXTEEN
The Day of the Pan Shining

The kitchen windows were always opened on pan-shining day. Saucepans of every size, cauldrons, colanders and frying pans were all brought down from their hooks on the high beams, and set out on the long kitchen table.

Dusters appeared from drawers and cupboards, tins of shine paste were carried up on trays from the Shaidi workshop, and all the Shaidi grandparents, aunts and uncles, Twig and her children got down on their knees and set to work dusting, polishing and shining.

A warm breeze blew in through the open windows, and scents of the forest mingled with lemon, honey and balsam.

It was one of those days at the end of March when you know that winter has begun to die, and spring is taking over.

Most of the household kept out of the kitchen on pan-shining day. The noise and the smells were too much for some, especially ex-witches with sensitive noses and extremely acute hearing. But Henry heard the enchanting music of pans and Shaidi singing, and couldn't resist a quick peek.

He stood in the open doorway, gazing at the lively bustle on the table, the piles of gleaming pans at one end, and those waiting to be polished at the other. A shadow fell across the scene. Henry thought it was a passing cloud, and then he saw it, and so did the Shaidi: a great grey thundercloud – the mayor's cat.

It sat looking in at them through the open window, and then it leapt over the big stone sink and on to the table. Amid the shrieks and screams of the little people, the monster cat paced down the centre of the table, sending pots and pans skittering and clanging.

The little folk leapt, flying off the table with dusters waving and aprons billowing; all but one. Bramble, stepping backwards, tripped on an upturned tin of paste and lay on her back before the dreadful creature.

'No!' screamed Henry. Seizing a saucepan, he flung it at the monster, hitting its one good eye. The great cat growled, showing its dreadful teeth. Henry leant across the table, frantically reaching for Bramble's hand, but the creature grabbed his wrist in its wicked jaws, and Henry yelled with pain. Great-aunts and uncles, grandparents and Twig and her children began to hurl anything they could lift: lids and pans, ladles and cleavers came flying at the monster cat. It let go of Henry's torn wrist, but stood its ground, growling defiance.

Thistle threw a knife at the hideous grey head, but it ducked and came on undeterred until it stood a few inches from Bramble's tiny foot.

A terrible wailing filled the room as the helpless Shaidi watched the youngest child struggling backwards while the monster continued its dreadful approach.

Desperately Henry lunged again, but he couldn't reach the tiny body. Something knocked against his head, and as he staggered sideways, a black shape sailed past him and landed on the monster's back.

'Enkidu!' gasped Henry, as his cat bit into the grey neck.

With a yowl of fury the monster shook his head, shook and shook until Enkidu rolled off. Henry could never accurately describe the fight that followed. It was so fast and furious. Black fur flew, grey fur flew, a tail lashed, claws gleamed, teeth tore into flesh, the growling and howling became a deafening cacophony.

Will it never end? Henry didn't know if the words were in his head or cried aloud. But, all at once, the monster turned and, racing up the table, bounded out through the open window.

Enkidu, crouching, battered on the table, one ear almost gone, a nose bitten and bloody, suddenly sped up the table and flew after the monster.

'No!' cried Henry. 'No, Enkidu. Let it go!'

It was no use. Enkidu couldn't let the monster live.

Racing for the back door, Henry and the Shaidi family tore into the garden. Henry, not caring if he was seen, leapt ahead of everyone with shorter legs. He reached the meadow and saw the tall grasses churning and thrashing. The cats fought in silence now, their business too deadly for any sounds, but as Henry sprinted through the grass towards them, there were two mournful howls, and then a stillness so deep and sudden it brought Henry to a standstill.

By the time he found the bodies, the Shaidi had caught up with him. They stood back, allowing Henry to approach the cats alone. Tears blurred his vision, but he could see how small his brave cat looked beside the mayor's monster.

Again and again Henry rubbed his eyes, but the tears kept falling, and he could hardly make out the terrible wounds on Enkidu's body. How still he lay, how quietly.

Henry fell to his knees beside his friend. He ran his hand across the long, soft fur and, for a moment, thought his heart had stopped, for how could he live without Enkidu? He lay his head on the silent body, and heard the thump of his heart again. And then another: *thump, thump,* slower and softer than his own. Enkidu's heart.

'His heart is beating!' cried Henry.

The little people ran to him, surrounding the two bodies, one quite dead, the other one alive. A tall figure strode through the grass behind them. Mr Lazlo had arrived.

Henry sat back while the Shaidi stroked the silky fur, touched the torn ears, felt the wounded body. Bramble lay her head against the injured nose and, in a voice choked with sobs, she said, 'We will make Enkidu better, won't we, Ma? Won't we, Grandpa?'

'We will, indeed,' said Thistle, 'but we must take him now. There's not a moment to lose if we're to keep that heart still beating. I fear the grey beast had poison on his claws.'

'I'll carry him,' said Mr Lazlo.

'No, no,' cried Henry. 'Don't take him away.'

But Mr Lazlo bent and gently lifted Enkidu into his arms. 'Let the Shaidi have him for a while,' he said. 'They know what to do.'

'They hate him!' wailed Henry.

'No, no, no,' came a chorus of soft voices.

'Enkidu risked his own life for us,' said Thistle solemnly. 'Bramble would most certainly have been killed if it wasn't for his bravery. We will never forget that. And we will do all in our power to save him.'

'And their power is considerable,' said Mr Lazlo.

So, Henry found himself following Mr Lazlo

through the trees and along the path to the green door, while the Shaidi whispered quietly all around him. He watched Mr Lazlo lay Enkidu in a bed of gossamer placed upon a wide tree stump, and then he put his own hand on Enkidu's side and, yes, his cat's heart was still beating.

'I'll stay while you . . . do what you have to do,' Henry told Thistle.

'No,' said the little man. 'It would be better if you returned tonight.'

'But I have to be with him,' Henry insisted.

'No,' Mr Lazlo said firmly. 'You must put your trust in Thistle and his family.'

'But . . . but . . .' Henry swayed from foot to foot.

Mr Lazlo placed a hand on his shoulder. 'Trust me, they will do what they have to do, and then you can see Enkidu again. You do trust me, don't you, Henry?'

'Yes,' said Henry.

With a last look at his friend, he left him in Thistle's care, and allowed Mr Lazlo to lead him back to the house. It was rather late to take precautions, but Mr Lazlo insisted that Henry keep close and walk in his shadow, just in case there were spies about.

'What about the other one?' Henry whispered. 'The mayor's cat?'

Mr Lazlo told him not to concern himself. The 'other one' would be dealt with.

When they got back to the house, they walked into a kitchen where children and Guardians had taken over the abandoned pan-shining.

Mark was crawling along a beam, hanging the polished pans back on their hooks, Lucy and Ankaret were dusting, Christian polishing, and Miss Notamoth was trailing her long sleeves over the undusted pans. Mrs Hardear was scolding Professor Pintail for polishing a cauldron with his beard, and the princess was fretting that the pans were not responding well to their unfamiliar shiners. 'They have lost their song,' she complained. 'Can't you hear it?'

'How can we hear a silent pan?' asked Marigold, ineffectually patting a ladle. And then she saw Henry and cried out his name.

Everyone stopped work and gaped at Henry and Mr Lazlo.

'Twig told us what happened before she ran after you,' cried Marigold. 'Oh, Henry, I'm so sorry. Herbert made us stay here while you . . . Enkidu is going to be all right, isn't he?'

Henry shrugged.

'A brave cat,' said Christian, and there were cries of agreement and many murmurs of comfort and sympathy. Their kindness brought a lump to Henry's throat. He might have wept if the princess hadn't come to his rescue by saying, 'I think you would like to be on your own for a while, Henry, isn't that so?'

Henry nodded, dumbly.

'I'll come and fetch you when the stars are out,' she said, 'and we'll visit Enkidu together.'

Henry nodded again, gratefully, and went up to his room to wait.

CHAPTER SEVENTEEN
Lucy's Whisperers

Henry sat on his bed. He tried to imagine his world without Enkidu. He had never belonged so completely to another living being, and he wondered if Enkidu's heart should fail, then, perhaps, his own would too. 'What shall I do?' he kept murmuring. 'What shall I do?'

'*Trust them,*' Mr Lazlo had said. '*Trust the Shaidi!*'

But Enkidu had looked so broken, so very still. What kind of magic could possibly save him?

Henry laid his head on the place at the end of the bed where Enkidu had always slept. He closed his eyes and began to wait.

Time passed. Henry didn't move. Dusk approached. The trees outside creaked and whispered. Night began to fall and the room grew dark. Henry went to the window, and was just in time to see Mr Lazlo mount his black stallion. Herbert stood by the open gates and watched Mr Lazlo ride into the forest. There was a grey sack hanging from the back of his saddle.

Henry didn't want to be alone any more. He trudged wearily down the tower steps to the kitchen.

It was suppertime. The pans had all been cleaned and hung shining from their hooks on the beams. It looked all too festive in Henry's opinion, all that sparkle, but then he couldn't expect everyone else's life to stop, just because his own had. There was a lull in the conversation when he went in, and he was aware of the sympathetic looks thrown in his direction, but he avoided meeting anyone's eye.

He took his usual place between Mark and Marigold. Marigold spoke his name, and Mark put a hand on his arm, but he couldn't look at them. A plate of fish pie was put before him, and he stared at it, reaching for his knife and fork without raising his eyes.

'Rover Henry!' said a small, sharp voice.

Henry took a moment to look up. Twig stood in front of him, holding a glass of green juice. Gazing earnestly into his face, she said, 'I want to thank you for bringing your cat into our house.'

'What?' Henry said dully. He couldn't quite believe his ears.

'Thank you,' said Twig again. 'Your cat is loyal and brave. He is steadfast and heroic. He saved my child's life and has avenged my dear husband, Moss.'

Henry gaped. He was impressed with Twig's little speech, but didn't know how to respond. It seemed that he didn't have to, for Twig had more to say.

'Our mortal enemy is dead, and my children's father smiles from his leafy bed. Enkidu will be fully recovered within a week, I promise.' Twig placed the glass of juice beside Henry's plate. 'Double strength,' she said, and, after making a little bow, she walked sedately back to the top of the table.

The drumming of tiny feet above Henry made him look up. Nut and Nettle, Mint and Marjoram, and even Bramble, were sitting in a row on the beam. As they drummed their feet against the wood, they clapped their hands and called, 'Hooray! Hooray for Enkidu!'

'Hooray!' echoed the cockatoo, from the back of the princess's chair.

Henry smiled at last. Everyone smiled. The ex-witches nodded fondly at him, and he quickly downed the green juice. Double strength tasted very bitter, but he was sure he felt a slight itch at the top of his scalp, where a new hair might be growing.

The fish pie was very good. The children gave it their full attention. There was no space for chatter. Mr Lazlo came in, looking a bit dusty, and soon afterwards, Henry was aware of an argument going on at the other end of the table. Henry didn't know how it had begun, but he heard Professor Pintail suddenly raise his voice and say, 'If we could use our skills, just once, Princess.'

'Or now and again,' Mrs Hardear suggested.

'Surely, no harm, would, er . . .' Miss Notamoth's voice trailed off.

'You know how I feel about it,' the princess said coldly.

'Just a suggestion, Princess,' said Herbert, winking at Mrs Hardear.

'And what could a duck, a moth, and a pair of ears achieve?' the princess asked scathingly.

The ex-witches looked slightly offended and returned to their suppers. Professor Pintail wouldn't give up, however. 'Our individual skills are limited, I'll admit,' he said, 'but together, Princess, together we could achieve much. We might have rescued Markendaya, instead of letting brave Henry travel through the night forest alone.'

'He wasn't alone,' the princess retorted.

'Not entirely,' the professor agreed, 'but –'

'Enough!' Flinging down her table napkin, the princess stood up and marched out of the room.

'Oh dear!' said the cockatoo.

'Now you've done it,' sighed Herbert.

'She'll come round,' said Mr Lazlo calmly.

'But will she come round to our point of view?' asked the professor.

Mr Lazlo shrugged. 'Past events, Professor. Past events weigh heavily.'

'Tch!' muttered the professor. 'Those people!' He gave an apologetic cough. 'Your people, I mean, Mr Lazlo. They were competing against each other. It's no wonder they vanished. We would be working together a very different matter, wouldn't you agree?'

'Entirely,' said Mr Lazlo. 'But let's not forget the cockatoo.'

'Accidents can happen,' Herbert said quietly, glancing at the cockatoo, 'when you're in a hurry.'

The meal continued in almost complete silence.

After supper when the other children had begun to clear the plates, Lucy moved into the seat beside Henry. He hadn't quite finished and was determined to eat every scrap, but he couldn't help glancing at his empty glass, now and again.

'It really does work, you know,' said Lucy.

'The green juice?'

'Yes, I'm the living proof. I was only five when I began to drink it. Now I'm twelve, and still growing.'

Henry was puzzled. 'Didn't you want to go home?'

'I am home,' said Lucy. 'I was born here.'

When she said this, Henry was sure that the walls around them creaked and sighed, and the shining pans shivered, their gentle music becoming cautious and melancholy.

'You were *born* here?' said Henry, not understanding. 'Do you mean that you have always lived in this house, and never left the forest?'

'Never.'

Henry put down his fork. 'You've never been to another town. Never seen the sea?'

'Never,' she repeated. 'Of course, I have been to Timeless many times. I accompany the princess when she goes shopping. She buys me clothes and books. I enjoy that.'

'But, Lucy,' Henry forgot his last mouthful, 'was there never a . . . a journey for you, like the rest of us? A journey through a marble?'

'Yes, there was a journey,' she said wistfully.

'But how?' Henry allowed Christian to remove his plate still containing that last precious mouthful. 'Tell me,' he said.

'Long before the criminals came, there was a village, where Timeless has grown. I lived here, with my family; the other children were older than me. Our name was Little, even though my father was tall and strong.' Lucy gave a small, sad smile. 'A terrible sickness came. They called it a plague. One by one my family died. My sister, the last to die, said, "Go to the village, Lucy, and you will be saved."'

'So you went through the forest?'

Lucy nodded. 'On my small pony. I knew there

were other creatures about me, I had always known they were there, in the forest, but I could never see them. No one was alive in the village, so I returned and waited to die. I was very sick when the Shaidi came out of the forest and cared for me. They saved my life. This house became their home and mine. They even changed the sign on the gate – just a bit.' She smiled. 'It used to be called Little Court.'

'The Shaidi,' Henry said thoughtfully. 'And the marble?' He turned his chair to face Lucy.

'I found it in a jar. I tipped it up and it rolled on to my hand.'

'And you looked into it,' said Henry.

'You know, don't you?' said Lucy. 'The wonder of it. The beautiful world. I wanted to stay there forever.'

'And then you came out?'

'Yes. Into this room. And there sat the princess.' She pointed to the end of the table. 'And there was Mr Lazlo and Herbert, and Miss Notamoth and Mrs Hardear and Professor Pintail and Twig.'

'What a shock for them.'

'For anyone else, maybe,' said Lucy, 'but because they are . . . different, they weren't horrified or anything. They listened to me, looked after me, taught me everything I know, and when I didn't grow, Twig and her family brewed and blended, and mixed and stirred until they had made a green juice. They gave it to me every day, and I grew. That was seven years ago.'

'And now you look like you're twelve.'

Lucy beamed. 'You see.'

Henry looked up at the shining pans. He gazed at the shelves of higgledy-piggledy china, and the tall topaz-coloured windowpanes. 'I think I can hear your family, sometimes, Lucy,' he said. 'But was this room just the same, when your second life began?'

'After several hundred years? Goodness, no. It was very changed, and yet I knew where I was. It felt familiar. And I could hear the voices of my brothers and sisters. I still can.' Lucy hunched her shoulders. 'But while I was lost in that marble, and the centuries passed, terrible things were happening to the Shaidi. People came with guns and axes, with swords and knives and with fire.' She frowned and twisted her hands together.

'I know,' said Henry, 'the princess told me.'

The room had emptied, all but for the children busy washing and drying at the sink.

'Why d'you think our journeys through the marbles were so different?' asked Henry. 'Yours lasted hundreds of years, Mark's only three months.'

Lucy gave a wry smile. 'I was told that they wre made a very long time ago, by the granddaughters of an African magician. Perhaps those girls wanted to make all the marbles different. Perhaps, to them, it was just a game.'

'What a game,' said Henry.

Lucy stood and, brushing down her skirt, said gravely, 'I'm glad that you can hear my family, Henry. I think the Shaidi brought their voices back to keep me company.'

'I sometimes think they're trying to keep me company too,' said Henry.

Lucy smiled. 'You will grow, Henry. And you will get home.'

'Yes, I will,' he said confidently, 'and Enkidu will get better.'

By the time they joined the others at the sink, the washing and drying had all been done.

'Just one spoon left,' said Marigold, tossing Henry a tea towel. 'A spoon for luck.'

The spoon had a tiny duck engraved at the end. Noticing Henry staring at the duck, Ankaret said, 'A pintail. A pintail duck, that is. It must be part of the professor's collection.'

Henry didn't pay much attention to Ankaret's remark. It was only later that he understood its significance.

Herbert offered Henry a room in the house for the night. There was no need for him to sleep alone in the tower, he said, now that his cat had proved to be a hero.

But Henry declined. He wanted to stay in the room that he and Enkidu had shared for so many nights.

He didn't attempt to get into bed. Instead he waited at the window; waited for the stars to show themselves. But a blanket of cloud lay above the forest, and Henry wondered if the princess had forgotten him, or changed her mind. After what must have been an hour, he decided it was time to visit Enkidu; he would go alone.

Henry put on the red anorak and crept down the winding stairway. He found the princess waiting for him in the passage. She was holding a large lantern that contained a fat, flickering candle.

'I thought you had forgotten,' said Henry.

'Of course not,' retorted the princess. 'You didn't expect me to climb all those steps, did you, at my age?'

Henry couldn't guess what the princess's age might be, so he said, 'I suppose not. But there are no stars.'

'There are stars, Henry,' said the princess, unlatching the back door. The bolts had already been drawn back, Henry noticed.

The door swung open and they stepped into the dark, starless night. *So much for stars,* thought Henry. But once they were through the mossy door in the wall, he was astonished to see a sky of glittering brilliance.

'We hardly need a lantern, do we?' said the princess, her free hand clasping Henry's.

Henry wondered if the princess took her rings off in bed. Her grip tightened as they stepped along the paved walk.

'When Lazlo was small,' said the princess in her gentle, library voice, 'he used to complain that my rings hurt his fingers. But my dear husband, the prince, told me always to wear them, in case everything else was lost. I often wonder if he guessed what would happen.'

'I think he did,' said Henry, trying not to mind the biting jewels.

'I wish I had a little boy again,' went on the princess. 'Perhaps a grandson,' she added wistfully. 'But Lazlo will never marry, never have a child of his own. He must stay here for the rest of his life.'

'Why?' said Henry. 'He could travel in the Shaidi coach. He could escape and see the world.'

'Dear Henry,' sighed the princess. 'The coach will only take you back to the place you call home. For Lazlo and me, that place lies a hundred miles under the snow. The Shaidi have tried to make the coach change direction, but it seems to be beyond their power.'

Never one to give up, Henry said, 'But someone might come in. A new witch, perhaps. A beautiful one. I'm not saying that Miss Notamoth and Mrs Hardear aren't beautiful, but Mr Lazlo doesn't seem to have fallen in love with them.'

The princess's silvery laugh rang across the meadow, sending the night owls, like flying ghosts, high into the trees.

'Will you send someone, Henry, when you get out?' she asked. 'A lady for Lazlo to love?'

Henry smiled. 'I'll try,' he said, and then he asked, 'How did the stars break through the cloud, Princess? There were none on the other side of the house.'

'The Shaidi have their ways,' she replied. 'But I won't pretend to understand them.'

'And I don't understand how they took the night forest back to the time when ghouls and goblins lived, and giants were taller than the trees.'

'Let's just be thankful that they can do such things.' The princess let go of Henry's hand and began to make her way through the long grass, while Henry followed, rubbing his ring-bruised fingers.

When they reached the green door, Henry hung back. The Shaidi's workroom had previously sent busy sounds humming out into the forest. Now it was silent.

'Why is it so quiet?' Henry whispered.

'Why do you think?' the princess replied.

'Not because . . .' Henry couldn't continue.

'Enkidu will not die, Henry. Come.' The princess opened the green door and Henry walked cautiously into the workroom.

The light was low, but the room was not silent. The Shaidi were chanting, their voices so soft they could barely be heard from the doorway. They were all seated on the ground beside the wide tree stump where Enkidu lay. Bramble sat at the head of the bed, leaning against the wood.

Thistle stood up when he saw Henry and the princess. He beckoned Henry, and the princess let him approach Enkidu alone. The big cat was lying on his side. He looked very peaceful. Strips of pale gossamer covered his wounds and his breath was calm and even.

'He looks better,' Henry whispered, and he put out a hand and touched the furry head.

At Henry's touch, Enkidu gave a quiet, but very distinct, purr.

'The first purr,' said Bramble in a hushed, excited voice. She stood on tiptoe and peered at Enkidu's face.

'He heard you, Henry,' said Thistle. 'Now, he will recover quickly.'

'Thank you,' breathed Henry. 'Thank you for saving him.'

'Come back tomorrow and his eyes will be open,' said Thistle.

Henry was allowed a little more time with his cat,

and then gently persuaded to go to bed.

A week passed. Every time that Henry saw Enkidu he had improved. His torn ear began to heal. He lapped up the medicine that swirled in tasty spring water, and rarely complained at the sweet-smelling paste applied to his wounds. He even appeared to enjoy the chanting. His eyes began to shine, and his fur took on a thick, glossy sheen.

On the tenth day, Thistle told Henry that soon his cat would be well enough to return to the house.

On the twelfth day, Marigold began to get ready for her second attempt at travelling home.

Also on the twelfth day the four Guardians with Christian and Lucy, set off in the trap, to fetch supplies from the town. Soon it would be Mark's turn. He was growing steadily and eager to get home and see his mother. Henry still showed no sign of growing. All he had was hope.

Henry had just returned from a visit to Enkidu when Ankaret came to see him in his room. She sat on the bed opposite Henry's and frowned at her swinging feet.

'He's getting better,' said Henry, hoping to cheer her up.

'Good.' Her feet stopped swinging. 'You belong together.'

'Yes,' said Henry.

'And you'll leave together.'

'I hope so.'

Ankaret's feet began to swing again, and her fingers twitched.

'You could come with me, Ankaret,' said Henry. 'I know the princess says the coach will only take you back to where you came from, but if we went together, perhaps it would take me home, take both of us to my home, not yours. Perhaps the Shaidi could make it work. You've grown. You'd be safe anywhere.'

'I'm safe here,' she said.

'But not happy.'

'Of course, I'm happy,' she said, her fingers drumming furiously on her knees.

'But there's no piano,' he said gently. 'No music of any kind.'

'The Shaidi sing.' Her voice was defiant but very soft and there were tears in her eyes.

'I'm sorry, Ankaret.' Henry felt guilty. 'I didn't mean to upset you. But we could try to go together.'

She remained silent for a while, and then she said, 'Suppose it doesn't work. Suppose we're shot down, or go to the wrong house. I'm afraid I might find myself back in that awful place, or even worse, at the pile of dust where Mum and Dad and my baby sister died.'

Henry didn't know what to say. How could he know what might happen next?

Indeed, what happened next was the last thing anyone expected.

Henry stood up and looked out of the window. There was a movement outside the gate; the colour of foxgloves. He screwed up his eyes and leant close to the window. There was no mistaking them now. Peter and Penny Reed were standing at the gate. Peter began to climb it.

'No!' gasped Henry.

Ankaret leapt up. 'What is it?'

'Find Mr Lazlo,' said Henry. 'Someone's trying to get in.'

They raced down the stairs. When they reached the passage, Ankaret ran to the kitchen while Henry went on to the back door.

'Henry, where are you going?' called Ankaret.

'I'm going to stop them,' he said.

'You can't! You can't! It isn't safe,' she cried.

'Just find Mr Lazlo,' begged Henry. 'Someone's got to stop them.'

What was he thinking? He certainly wasn't thinking clearly. What was on his mind, as he dashed for the chair, climbed on it, unbolted the door, lifted the latch and raced down the path?

Perhaps Enkidu was on his mind, perhaps it was the Shaidi in their secret workroom, or Marigold preparing for her second journey.

Henry reached the gate. Clutching the ironwork, he shook it violently.

Peter had almost climbed to the top. Looking down at Henry, he said, 'Hullo! We wondered where you had got to.'

And then everything went very, very dark.

CHAPTER EIGHTEEN
Trapped

Henry had a bad headache. He was in a box, a tin box, by the sound of it, because when he moved his foot, there was a metallic clang. It was difficult to breathe and he wondered if he was in a coffin.

'This is kidnapping,' Henry cried in a dry voice.

His cry was greeted with laughter. Henry made out the voices of two men and two children.

'You won't get away with it,' Henry croaked.

There was more laughter and Penny Reed called out, 'But we have got away with it.'

'I bet there's a big bruise on your head,' Peter shouted, close to Henry's ear.

'That was my stone,' Penny sang out. 'Straight through the patterns in the gate.'

'They don't call her Dead-eye Penny for nothing,' said Peter.

Henry was tempted to say something rude, but decided to save his breath. He could hear the burr of an engine and imagined that his box lay on the floor of an open trailer. Peter and Penny seemed to be sitting each side of him, but he couldn't hear the other voices properly above the sound of the engine.

Henry wriggled and kicked, but his efforts only produced more laughter. After some time the engine stopped and he felt his box being lowered and then lifted.

'Goodbye, Henry,' called Peter and Penny.

Henry didn't bother to reply. A door opened and he was carried for a while before another door creaked open. He slid forwards as the box was tilted downwards. Bracing himself as best he could against the sides of his container, he heard two pairs of heavy footsteps thumping down a flight of stone steps.

'Ow!' cried Henry as his knees and elbows were thrown against the metal. A few paces on from the bottom step, a heavy key was turned in a lock and another door slowly opened; this one groaned as it scraped along the hard floor.

Henry's box was carried past the door and then dropped just beyond it. When the box hit the floor the impact shook Henry's bones, from his skull to his toes. He gave a loud groan and a deep voice told him to shut up or there'd be worse.

How could there be worse? Henry wondered, and then he thought, *Well, of course there could.*

The door clanged shut. The heavy footsteps receded and Henry was left, aching in every part of his body. He lay as still as he could, hoping the pain would soon fade.

He thought he was alone, so when someone spoke it gave him quite a shock.

'Welcome, Henry!' The voice was familiar; it was a man's voice, high and harsh.

Henry couldn't help himself. 'That's a silly thing to say,' he grunted, 'considering how I've been treated.'

'So far, I agree,' said the man. Henry could place the voice now, and he gritted his teeth. It was the mayor. 'Let's get you out of there, shall we?'

There was a click on Henry's right side and the lid of his tin coffin swung open. He looked up into the mayor's ashy-coloured face. The man bent over and peered down, his wispy hair hanging lifelessly from under his wide-brimmed hat, his breath like sour milk.

'Want a hand?' The mayor extended warty fingers.

'No,' said Henry. Clutching the sides of the box he pulled himself up and, with his feet still in the box, looked around the room he found himself in.

It could have been worse. Henry had expected a dusty cellar, but the brick walls had been painted white, and there was a rush mat on the floor. He could see the sky through the bars of a small, high window, but the truckle bed beneath it looked narrow and hard. It was covered in a grey blanket. There was a wooden screen in one corner, and Henry could easily imagine what it concealed.

There were two upright wooden chairs, one on each side of the tin box.

'Take a seat, Henry.' The mayor pointed to one of the chairs. 'No point in standing, when we've so much to discuss.'

Henry, still feeling shaky, stepped out of the box and quickly sat down. The mayor took the other chair. He said, 'Tell me what you were doing at the princess's house.'

'Nothing. I'd just got there,' said Henry.

'Really?' The mayor screwed up his narrow eyes. 'But you ran away from those nice Reeds weeks ago.'

'I lived in the forest,' said Henry. 'I learnt bush craft when I was a Scout.' He wondered if the mayor knew a lie when he heard one.

'And at night?' The mayor put his elbows on his bony knees and rested his chin on his hands.

'I slept in the trees,' Henry said evenly.

'In the trees?' The mayor pulled on one end of his meagre moustache. 'I'm told you had a black and white cat.'

Henry clenched his fists. Hoping the mayor hadn't noticed, he said, 'Yes. He ran away. I don't know where he went.'

'I do.' The mayor leant forwards and stared into Henry's eyes. 'I saw him in the princess's house.'

'Did you?' Henry feigned surprise. 'He must have climbed in somewhere, looking for food. He wasn't there when I . . . when I got to the house.'

They stared at each other. The mayor rubbed his shoulder and said, 'I had a cat. A lovely, big, cuddly cat. My Dear One. He kept me warm.'

Henry hesitated before asking, 'Where is he now?'

The mayor shrugged. His mouth drooped along with his moustache. 'Something in the forest got him, I shouldn't wonder. There are monsters in the forest. Perhaps you saw them?'

Henry swallowed and said, 'No. Well, maybe. It's very dark in there.' After several silent seconds he asked, 'What are you going to do with me?'

'Do with you?' The mayor grimaced.

Henry spoke in a rush. 'Are you going to keep me here, or send me away?' He suddenly realised this was impossible.

For the first time since they'd met, the mayor looked happy. 'Silly boy! Send you away? We can't. No one can leave Timeless, no one. Now you're in, you're in for good.'

Henry said nothing.

'You're here to be observed, Henry,' said the mayor. 'We had information from outside, you see, that children were being found – children who do not grow. We believe that three have turned up here, including you, Henry. All found by the clever Reeds. A boy and a girl were lost, but now we have our own little un-grown boy, and we'll make quite sure that you are not lost.'

Henry looked away from those very pale eyes. *So he doesn't know about Marigold and Ankaret,* he thought.

'You will be observed, Henry,' repeated the mayor, 'and on the next equinox, I'll get word to the outside. Let them know the results of our initial observations, with notes and photographs.'

'But how did those people "outside" discover that you were here?' Henry asked.

The mayor regarded his yellow fingers and said, 'Long ago, a great-uncle of mine came looking for us. Quite by chance he chose the equinox, and when he heard that he would be trapped, he ran for the exit and, to the town's great surprise, got out. Later, extraordinary power came to this uncle – by fair means or foul, who knows.' Here, the mayor gave an unpleasant chuckle. 'But his relatives have never forgotten that a small part of their family is trapped here, inside a forest.'

The mayor chuckled again, slapped his knee, and winced.

Henry found himself staring at the curiously misshapen knee protruding from the mayor's baggy trouser leg.

'Stare all you want,' the mayor said savagely. 'Soon my knees will be as smooth and pink as yours. Because I'll have your blood, Henry. I'll take it, drop by drop, until I'm full of it. Full of you. I'll be a youth again, and I'll never, never grow old. What d'you think of that?'

What could Henry think? He was filled with a cold dread and gazed at his hands, already imagining them drained of blood and white as chalk, or would they be as grey as veined marble.

The mayor stood up and pushed back his chair. 'You'll get a meal later. There's a toilet and a basin behind that screen. We'll have another chat tomorrow.' He limped to the door. His breathing was harsh and he rubbed his shoulder constantly.

There was nothing in the room except for the bed, the chairs and the tin box. Henry was alone with his thoughts. He missed Enkidu more than he could have imagined. For now, he realised, he might never see him again. Was it possible to be kept in one room for the whole of your life? Henry couldn't believe it.

He climbed on the bed and looked out of the window. A bare, bleak field spread before him, almost as far as he could see. On the horizon a line of trees: the forest, part of the Shaidi's enchanted wall. Henry watched the sky darken, the first stars appear and the grey mist of dusk cover the field.

He was still standing on the bed when a key turned

in the lock and the door scraped open. A henchman walked in, carrying a tray. He kicked the lid of the metal box and it closed with a bang. In silence the man placed the tray on the tin lid. Water slopped over the rim of a thick earthenware mug, a candle flickered, and a sandwich slid off a metal plate.

The man didn't even glance at Henry as he marched out. His polished boots and gold insignia gleamed dully in the weak light, and then he was gone.

So they're not going to starve me, thought Henry. *They want a nice, healthy un-grown boy for their investigations.* And then it occurred to him that perhaps he would grow. Perhaps soon the effects of the double-strength green juice would show. Surely, then, he would be free?

The sandwich had meat in it and tasted quite good, but the water was warm and smelt stale. When he had finished his meal, Henry placed what was left of the candle beside his bed, visited the toilet and climbed under the grey blanket. For a while he lay awake, reliving his dreadful day, and then he began to yawn. Gradually he drifted off to sleep.

When Henry woke up, dawn light was filtering through the bars on the window, and he could just make out a figure sitting beside the tin box. The mayor was back.

Henry felt ill. He hadn't had breakfast and here

came an interrogation. He pretended he was still asleep but the mayor must have seen him open his eyes.

'Good morning, Henry. Time for another chat.'

The chilly voice tugged Henry awake. He dragged himself over to the other chair and slumped on to it.

'Why did you come here, Henry?' The words were clipped and cold.

Henry almost blurted out the truth, but stopped himself just in time. 'My aunt brought me,' he said simply.

'We know that.' The mayor spat out the words. 'But why? Why did she leave you here and whizz off within the hour, probably knowing that you could never leave?'

Henry shrugged.

The mayor slapped his knees and screeched, 'Why?'

'I think she . . . she made a mistake,' said Henry. 'We sort of got lost, and found this cafe, and while I was having some chips, she remembered she'd left a cake in the oven, and dashed home, and couldn't get back to fetch me.'

'You make me sick,' said the mayor with a nasty sneer. 'You can't even tell a lie properly. But I'll get the truth out of you.'

Henry stared at the barred window.

'In the meantime,' went on the mayor, 'we shall watch you, even while you sleep. And we shall make a fortune for observing a phenomenon. Why, you might live to be a hundred years old, and still look only ten.'

This last remark made Henry's head spin. He began to shiver. 'But I am growing,' he said faintly.

'Come now, tell the truth.'

'I'm growing,' said Henry, mustering a bit of defiance.

'If you say so.' The mayor got up. 'After your breakfast you'll be weighed and measured. Notes will be kept. Every single day of the rest of your life will be recorded.'

The mayor had been making for the door. He stopped in his tracks and, all at once, looked sullen. 'We'll talk again.' As he left the room he looked back and said viciously, 'Where's my cat, Henry?'

'How should I know?' Henry gave what he hoped was a clueless shrug.

The mayor slammed the door, and Henry heard him groan, 'Ugh! My arm!'

A few moments later a henchman walked in with a glass of milk and a bowl of cereal. The milk spilt when he slammed it on the tin box, but Henry was past caring. The cereal tasted of sawdust.

It was difficult to know if it was the same henchman who came in half an hour later. They wore their helmets so low on their foreheads, most of their features were hidden or in shadow. The man picked up the tray containing Henry's empty cup and glass, the bowl and the plate, and left the room with an unfriendly grunt.

Henry was standing on his bed, looking at the distant forest, when his third visitor appeared. It was someone totally unexpected, and horribly familiar.

'Good morning,' said the man, setting down a large black bag. 'I've come to weigh and measure you.'

'You!' said Henry incredulously.

'I'm a doctor,' said the man Henry knew as Mr Reed. 'I probably forgot to mention it.'

'Yes,' Henry mumbled.

The doctor opened his bag, took out several unpleasant-looking instruments and laid them on the tin box. 'Come here, please.'

Henry got off the bed and stood before the doctor. He tried not to show it, but his knees were shaking.

'Nothing to it, Henry,' Dr Reed said coldly. 'Put out your tongue.'

In a daze, Henry obeyed.

After his throat was examined, Henry was weighed. His feet were measured, his head, arms, waist, fingers, nails, hair – every bit of him, in fact, was pinched, prodded, measured and then recorded in a black book.

When all this had been done, Dr Reed packed his machines and instruments back into his bag and left, saying, 'I'll see you tomorrow, and we'll take some blood.'

CHAPTER NINETEEN
The Tempest

Henry had always been an optimist. He was forever telling himself that things could be worse. But there comes a time when even an optimist begins to believe that their life is definitely going downhill; a time when they begin to lose hope. This happened to Henry when he'd been in the locked room for almost three weeks. They had cropped his hair very short and his arms were pitted with needle pricks from the blood tests he'd been subjected to.

There was nothing to do all day, and he found it hard to sleep at night; his head was cold and his arms throbbed. He had asked for a pencil and paper and this had been provided, so every day Henry marked his paper with a short line, and after four days he would put a fifth line through all the others. He'd read that prisoners in past times did this, and he was certainly a prisoner.

Every day Dr Reed would visit him and carry out the

undignified measuring and weighing business. Henry's head would be scrutinised through a magnifying glass, and then a photograph would be taken. At the end of every examination, the doctor would give a cool smile and say bluntly, 'No change. No growth.'

When the doctor had gone Henry would stare at his nails, run his fingers through his hair and mutter. 'But I am growing. I must be. I drank the green juice.'

The mayor didn't put in another appearance for some time. Perhaps he had been waiting for Henry to weaken. On his next visit he looked meaner and more determined than ever. They sat on opposite sides of the tin box, just as they had before, but this time the mayor folded his arms across his chest, leant back and half-closed his eyes before barking, 'No lies, this time. Why did you come to Timeless, Henry?'

'My aunt brought me,' Henry said, once again.

'We know that,' the mayor snarled. 'But why? Why did she leave you here and whizz off within the hour? We know it wasn't because of a burnt cake, that's just not good enough.'

Henry shrugged.

The mayor slapped his knee, winced, and screeched, 'Why?'

Henry shrugged again.

'There must be a reason, a very good reason. The same thing happened to another boy, and a girl before that. But we lost them, lost them both.' The mayor wrinkled his nose and gave an unpleasant grin, revealing a row of long, horribly crooked teeth.

Henry dared to ask, 'How did you lose them?'

The mayor eyed Henry suspiciously. 'They ran away. Into the night forest, one in a lightning strike. They became meat for wolves, probably. So how come you survived?'

'I told you, I slept in the trees, and anyway, I went in daylight.'

'Didn't you like living with those nice Reeds?'

'No, I did not,' Henry said vehemently. 'There's still a bump on my head. Penny Reed did that. They're all horrible.'

'What?' screeched the mayor. 'They're my relatives. Best family in town. Reed is a brilliant doctor, completely self-taught.'

'So he's not a proper doctor,' Henry ventured.

'Of course he is. Excellent metal-work.' The mayor's face twisted into a smirk of irritation, and he left the room rubbing his shoulder.

On the mayor's next visit Henry changed his tune a little. When asked why he had been left alone in Timeless, Henry replied, 'I suppose I wasn't wanted. It's a good place to leave someone, isn't it, if you want to get rid of them?'

This surprised the mayor. When he left he looked

222

thoughtful rather than exasperated.

So Henry stuck to this story. He wasn't wanted. He was a freak without a family. His aunt must have heard of this strange place that you couldn't escape from, unless you left on the equinox, within the hour; a perfect place to a leave a boy who wasn't wanted.

Henry could see that the mayor was beginning to believe this explanation. The trouble was, Henry had to repeat his story so often, he almost began to believe it himself. No one had come to rescue him. But then, how could they without betraying themselves, and the Shaidi?

Every night Henry would put on a pair of ill-fitting grey pyjamas and climb under the coarse grey blanket. He began to dream of a boy growing old in a cold, white room without friends, without conversation or games, or even a book to read, and he would wake up shivering and dreading the day ahead.

The storms began towards the end of the third week. The rumble of thunder above the town was almost incessant; at night sheets of lightning spread across the sky, and blue sparks struck the earth, burning the grass into sooty patches of dust.

After two days the thunder rolled away and then the rain came; rain so heavy it drummed its way through roofs, poured into windows, flooded the drains and turned roads into rivers.

Clouds, like giant sacks of coal, lay across the town, barely higher than the roofs, and turning daylight into dusk. Henry's two visitors looked weary and anxious. Their nights were now as bad as his.

And then the wind arrived, and the citizens of Timeless wondered if they should be preparing for the end of the world. They had heard of hurricanes, of typhoons and tornadoes. But this wind was different. It turned the rain into icy missiles, it hurled giant branches into the streets, broke windowpanes with leaves of stone. Some said it was the forest, at war with them again.

Henry watched the tempest from his small window. He saw the trees on the horizon, swaying like river-reeds. *It's as if they're possessed*, he thought, *or under a spell*. He had no visitors that day. Even his supper was forgotten. Having nothing else to do, he stayed on his bed, watching the beaten, muddy field and the waving trees. And as he watched, something extraordinary happened. In the distance parts of the field began to rise. It was as if giant moles were tunnelling beneath the mud. The huge tunnels drew closer and closer, and suddenly Henry knew they were coming to him – for him.

Here and there, great ropes of wood lifted out of the ground, only to plunge back again, and then they were beating against the wall where Henry stood. He jumped off the bed as great gnarled tree roots burst into the room. Half the wall collapsed, and Henry stared out at a muddy bank – and freedom.

'Come on, Henry,' said a voice. 'Hurry up. We haven't got all night.'

Henry clambered over the roots and hauled himself to the top of the bank.

'That's right,' said the voice. 'Come on.'

Rolling on to the wet grass Henry looked all round, calling, 'Where are you? Where are you?'

'Here. Come on, follow me.'

Henry recognised the voice. But the only living thing he could see was a duck; a very handsome duck with a long pointed tail.

'Yes, it's me.' The duck gave a very human chuckle and said, 'Good disguise, eh? Come on!'

The duck began to waddle, very fast, along a path at the edge of the field. For the first time Henry could see his prison from the outside. It was a tall, grey building with few windows. In the wall beside Henry, long cracks ran from the roof to the ground, and in several places bricks had fallen out and lay scattered across the path.

'Glad you weren't hurt, boy,' said the duck. 'It was touch and go, wasn't it?'

'It was, Professor,' said Henry.

They reached a road, or rather a stream, rippling over cobblestones.

'Ah, water!' said the duck, jumping in the air. He landed in the stream with a splash, soaking Henry's pyjamas. His feet were bare and the wind was icy.

'Come on, come on,' said Professor Pintail. 'Mr Lazlo's waiting.'

The cobbled road appeared to run round the outskirts of the town. Henry could hear shouting in the distance. Horns blared and sirens wailed, but no one appeared on the road.

'It's almost dark,' said a husky voice. Not the professor's this time.

Henry looked up. A large brown moth fluttered over his head.

'Yes, it's me,' said Miss Notamoth. 'Hullo, Henry, dear.'

Henry stopped, his mouth dropped open and he stared at the moth.

'No, don't stop,' said Miss Notamoth. 'We must hurry. It's getting dark.'

'But . . . but . . .' Henry continued to splash through the cold, bubbling water. 'What happened? How did you? I mean, the storm, the trees, was it all you?'

'The princess allowed us to use our skills, just this once,' said the duck.

'She's become very fond of you, Henry,' said the

moth. 'Well, we all have. She was angry about what happened to you. Very angry.'

'So she let us do our bit, as it were,' said the duck. 'It was very satisfying to use fire and the dark mirror again.'

'And Herbert's ebony baton,' added the moth.

'It was Mr Lazlo who brought it all together,' said the duck. 'He is more powerful than any of us, and his skill with the language of enchantments is truly a marvel.'

'We had to work with the Shaidi, of course.' The moth hovered in front of Henry, before settling on his shoulder. 'They have access to the trees, and they were so, so anxious to help. You've become quite a favourite, Henry.'

Henry smiled into the rain and the moth disappeared under his pyjama collar. 'I can't abide water,' she said in a muffled voice.

Henry had to ask, 'But why are you . . .?

'A duck and a moth?' The professor waggled his elegant tail. 'We are what we are. We move back and forth. But we haven't used our real skills since the cockatoo fiasco. Mistakes are easily made.' The duck put on a sudden spurt. He spread his wings and began to fly above the stream.

'And can you get your proper shapes back?' Henry panted as he tried to keep up with the duck.

'Of course,' said the duck. 'Though I don't know what

my proper shape is any more. And I don't really mind.'

'Me neither,' whispered the moth.

Henry wondered what they meant by the cockatoo fiasco, but he was too exhausted to ask any more questions. He plodded on in silence, while the duck flapped encouragingly in front of him.

Thunder rumbled in the distance, but its groan had weakened and the rain was merely a damp mist. They rounded a bend in the road, and Henry's spirits leapt when he saw the forest only a short distance before them.

'We're safe,' he breathed.

'Close,' said the moth.

Not close enough. When Henry heard heavy thuds on the road behind him, he thought the thunder had returned, but the sounds had a horribly familiar ring; the dreadful tramp of iron-studded boots. He tried to run, but his heart was in his throat and he could hardly breathe.

'HALT.' The voice was deep, almost inhuman.

A violent shaking overcame Henry. Shrugging into himself, he bent his head while the words struck his back. 'DID YOU THINK THAT YOU COULD ESCAPE, HENRY YEWBEAM?'

Henry closed his eyes, and helplessly clenched his fists.

'THE MAYOR NEEDS YOU, HENRY, NEEDS YOUR BLOOD!'

CHAPTER TWENTY
The Wizard

There was a sudden whir of wings and Henry opened his eyes to see the duck soar over his head. In horror he turned as the duck flew, shrieking, straight at the henchmen, three of them, standing shoulder to shoulder, like a sinister grey wall.

The duck furiously attacked the iron helmets; he pecked the great padded shoulders and thick sleeves. But he couldn't avoid the vicious clubs forever.

When the first strike hit the duck's head, he gave a squark of pain and tilted away. He dived again and a second blow caught his wing, the third beat down on the pintail's slender neck and, with a pitiful croak, he fell at the henchmen's feet.

One of the men lifted a shining boot and Henry, jolted into rage, rushed at the grim, grey wall, not caring if he lived or died when he met those murderous clubs.

Rage was boiling in his ears, and he never heard

the clatter of hooves behind him. He only saw the henchmen throw back their heads, as if they were searching the heavens, and he stared in amazement as, with a deafening crack, their weapons shattered into a thousand pieces; their helmets burst apart, their long boots crumbled and the three bodies bent and tumbled. In a few seconds they were little more than piles of dust and stone.

Half-afraid to see what had caused such powerful magic, Henry forced himself to turn, and saw the great head of the black stallion. From his lofty height, Mr Lazlo smiled down at Henry.

'Just in time, eh, Henry?' he said with a gleam in his eye.

'Yes,' Henry whispered.

A tiny voice from under his collar, whined, 'Poor, poor professor.'

'Bring him to me,' the wizard commanded.

Henry lifted the pintail's poor limp body and, carrying it carefully, brought it to Mr Lazlo.

'I think his neck is broken,' Henry's tears fell freely. 'He was so brave.'

Mr Lazlo took the duck and, cradling him in one arm, gently stroked the feathers of his head. 'Come on, old man. You're not finished yet,' he said. And then, from the wizard came a voice that might have been the rush of a breeze, the sighing of trees, and the soft notes of many animals.

The quiet and mysterious sounds made Henry feel quite drowsy, but his eyes never left the motionless pintail. At last he saw a wing flutter. The long tail quivered and, slowly, the speckled head lifted.

'Close shave,' wheezed the duck.

'Indeed, you brave old man,' said Mr Lazlo.

The professor cleared his throat and coughed. 'Shall I take my other form?'

'Better hang on as you are for now,' said Mr Lazlo. 'It'll be an easier ride.'

'Righto!' To Henry's amazement, the duck stretched out his wings and flew over Mr Lazlo's head, landing on the horse's broad rump.

'Now for you, Henry!' With one arm Mr Lazlo lifted Henry on to the saddle behind him. 'Hold tight,' he said, 'it might be a rough ride.'

Henry clung to Mr Lazlo's broad waist. He could feel the duck, warm against his back, and he closed his eyes as the forest began to enfold them in its enchanted air.

If it was a rough ride Henry wasn't aware of it. Sometimes he awoke to hear the squeaks and shrieks of beasts and goblins, sometimes he glimpsed fiery eyes and giants' legs, but he merely clasped Mr Lazlo tighter, and felt safe again.

The gates of the Littles' house were open. They

galloped through and the stallion stood snorting into the night. The front door opened and the princess ran out.

'Henry! Dear Henry,' she cried.

He swung himself down from the black horse and the princess took him in her arms, crushing him against her sequinned dress. 'What have they done to you?' she demanded. 'Your poor, poor head. Did they torture you?'

'I'm all right, now,' he said, pulling away from the sequins.

The princess grabbed his hand. 'Quickly,' she said. 'The coach is ready. You must leave now!'

'But the moon?' Henry looked into the sky.

'No need to wait for the moon,' said the princess, speeding up.

Breathless, Henry was led through the garden, his feet tingling, his pyjamas soaked.

'You'll soon be warm and dry,' the princess told him. 'And then you'll be home.'

The Shaidi workroom was bright with candlelight, and Henry found that almost everyone was there.

'We've come to say goodbye,' said Lucy, giving him a hug.

'I'll miss you,' said Christian, patting Henry's shoulder.

'We'll all miss you,' said Mrs Hardear, her long arms

almost choking the life out of him. Henry was glad to see that she was still herself, and not just a pair of ears.

A black shape suddenly hurtled out of the crowd towards Henry. It hit his legs and gave a powerful miaow.

'Enkidu!' cried Henry, lifting his cat in a giant hug. He had to bury his head in the thick fur to hide a tear.

Enkidu looked magnificent. Every part of him was healed and shining.

'Thank you,' Henry murmured. 'Thank you, Shaidi.'

'It was nothing,' said Thistle. 'We did what had to be done. The thanks are all ours.'

'Yes, yes,' said the rest of his family. 'The thanks are all ours.'

Henry looked round at the beaming faces: Elm and Bee, Aspen, Burdock and Comfrey. And there was Twig, surrounded by her five children. Bramble gave him a shy little wave.

'Suppose they come here?' said Henry, all at once afraid for everyone. 'The mayor and his henchmen. They caught me at your gate.'

The princess gave one of her light, tinkling laughs. 'They will find nothing, Henry. You will all be gone. And the mayor will need Mr Lazlo's treatment more than ever, after that storm.'

Henry still felt anxious. 'But the Shaidi, this

wonderful workroom. They'll search. What if they find it?'

'The forest will hide them,' said the princess.

'This place will vanish into the trees,' said Twig. 'Temporarily, of course.'

'And we'll be tiny as fireflies,' added Bramble.

There was a sudden commotion in the doorway. Herbert and Mr Lazlo had arrived, looking determined.

Ankaret stood between them, twisting her hands nervously. Her hair had been brushed and framed her pale face in a shining copper cloud. She was wearing a buttercup yellow dress, and Henry thought she looked quite beautiful.

'Ankaret!' he exclaimed. 'Are you coming with me?'

'What happened to your hair?' she responded. 'And what on earth are you wearing?'

'Pyjamas. I didn't have time to change.'

Ankaret took a few more hesitant steps into the room. 'Suppose we go to the wrong place?' she said.

'You won't,' the princess told her. 'Henry's love for his home and his family is very strong. Hold his hand, and you'll get to the right place. You are both growing now, and all will be well.'

Henry's face fell. In all the excitement he'd forgotten the most important thing of all. Gently lowering Enkidu to the ground, he said, 'But I haven't grown.'

'Of course you have,' said the princess. 'You have taken the green juice – double strength, and it never fails.'

'But the doctor told me there were no signs at all.'

'Silly man,' said Twig. 'Bramble's eyes are the sharpest, and she knows you well, Henry. She will tell you.'

Bramble immediately scrambled on to the tree-table beside Henry. 'I have often looked into your eyes,' she said. 'We must look again.'

Henry bent to meet her gaze. Bramble's bright, dark eyes moved slowly up to his eyelids, along the rim below his eyes, and then up to his eyebrows.

'Yes,' she breathed. 'Your eyelashes are growing, your eyebrows have grown. You are different, Henry. You *have* begun to grow.' She clapped her tiny hands, and a murmur of relief ran round the room.

'I shall miss you both,' Bramble whispered. 'You and Enkidu.'

'And we'll miss you,' said Henry, 'but we'll find a way to see you again.'

'Yes,' she agreed.

'Ready?' The princess took the children's hands. Ankaret squared her shoulders and gave a cautious nod.

Henry almost lost his nerve. He looked out at the expectant, smiling faces. Two were missing. 'Marigold and Mark,' he said. 'I wanted to tell them goodbye.'

235

'They've gone already,' Ankaret said. 'But I know where they are.' She patted her pocket.

'Their journeys were successful,' the princess reassured him.

'There's just one thing I have to know before I go,' said Henry. He had noticed the cockatoo, perched on a high branch.

'Yes?' said the princess, a little impatiently.

'Who is the cockatoo?'

There was a sharp intake of breath as Herbert and Mrs Hardear exchanged glances.

'The cockatoo was a girl called Flora,' said the princess.

'We had to hide her quickly,' Mrs Hardear explained.

'One of our little mistakes,' added the duck, flying on to Herbert's shoulder. 'She was very fond of parrots. It was her idea.'

'And she is very happy,' said the princess. 'Now, come along.' She led them further into the room.

And there was the coach.

Henry gasped. It was beautiful, but so very small. The red and gold leaves that covered it glittered like jewels, the tiny windows were as clear and delicate as ice. A toffee-coloured pony stood in the traces, its flowing mane almost as long as its tail. It was no bigger than Enkidu.

'Stand here, both of you,' Thistle suddenly commanded. 'Now for the juice and the robes. We have no time for the usual long preparation. It must be done immediately, while the pony is at his best.'

Henry and Ankaret were made to stand beside two tree-tables. Here they were handed glasses of a sparkling red juice. Enkidu had a saucerful. He lapped it up eagerly, while Henry and Ankaret drank theirs. The juice tasted sharp and spicy. Henry could feel it moving through him like a hot wire. His toes and fingers tingled, his scalp felt as though it was shrinking. He hoped he wasn't being turned into an ant.

The children stared at each other as the little people climbed onto the tables, carrying swathes of glistening gossamer. Then the dressing began. The robes were as soft as thistledown. They floated over the children's heads and began to cling to their bodies. Next came the cloaks, the hoods soft as feathers, settled round their faces and Henry felt as if he were falling asleep and already dreaming.

He looked down at Enkidu and couldn't help smiling. His big cat was as small as a mouse, a mouse in a snow white cloak. When he looked up again, he was shocked to see Elm grinning down at him. He was as small as a little Shaidi. Before he could say a word he was being lifted into the golden coach, now, apparently, the usual size for a coach. Ankaret was already there, sitting on a red cushion with Enkidu beside her. Henry squeezed in next to his cat. He took Ankaret's hand and held it tight.

They heard a light creak above them as Thistle climbed into the driving seat. He gave a soft call in an unfamiliar, lilting language, and they slowly rose into the air.

Henry looked out at the crowd of smiling faces. The Shaidi were all standing on the tables and waving madly. Bramble was jumping up and down and clapping her hands. Henry just had time to notice that her bootlaces were tied, before he lost sight of them all, and the coach was sailing past the treetops, and then out into the night sky.

As the coach tilted, Henry looked down on the forest. So many trees. He wished he knew all their names. The canopy rippled like a wave, its colours – silver, grey, dark green and lily white – all softened by starlight.

The forest faded from view and they flew higher. Higher and higher. They lost the starlight and the moon, but tiny lights glittered from the roof of the coach and they could see each other's anxious faces. On and on they went, into a darkness whose icy fingers crackled against the windowpanes.

Henry thought of Thistle and the little pony, out in the freezing air. Could they survive?

The coach rocked. It whirled and jolted, and then came to a juddering halt.

'It's changed its mind,' cried Ankaret. 'It's going to take me back because my heart lies under the ground where my family died.'

Henry felt her hand slipping from his grasp and gripped it tighter. 'Wherever we go we'll be together,' he said, 'and I'll make sure you come home with me.'

Ankaret's face was impassive, her fingers limp.

'Believe me, Ankaret,' Henry implored. 'Say it, say you believe me.'

'I believe you,' she whispered.

'Good!' Henry thought of the white house on the cliff; he saw Pearl's kind and cheerful face, he pictured Charlie, laughing, as he so often did. And then he imagined Ankaret, standing in the meadow behind the house.

The coach seemed to sigh and, slowly, it began to move. The children felt themselves dropping. Lower and lower and, looking down through the windows, they saw the lights of a small town. They flew over parks and rivers, towns and cities, all twinkling and flashing below, like so many tiny fires.

Ankaret smiled. 'How beautiful the world is,' she said.

'Yes,' Henry agreed. 'And we're going home.'

'Will they like me, your people?'

'Of course they will,' said Henry. 'Everyone will like you.'

'And will I like them, Henry?'

Ankaret's fingers tapped nervously against his hand, and he knew she was playing a tune.

'You will definitely like them,' said Henry. 'Especially Charlie. Everyone likes Charlie. And there is a piano.'

They slept for a while, and when they woke up, the sun had begun to rise.

They climbed above the clouds and, for a moment, the earth was lost to them. Henry was beginning to wonder if they would ever see land again when the coach suddenly dived towards the ground and he lost his grip on Ankaret's hand. The doors flew open and the children tumbled into a meadow, their limbs tingling as their bodies stretched to their former size. They were in the field behind Ocean View.

Enkidu lay across Henry's stomach.

The children began to laugh. They looked at each other, wrapped in glittering robes and laughed so much their lungs began to ache.

Two figures ran towards them from the white house on the cliff. Aunt Pearl and Charlie.

'You're here! You're here, at last,' cried Charlie. 'You look like a ghost, but you're really here.'

'We're not ghosts,' said Henry. 'Charlie, meet

Ankaret.'

'Hi, Ankaret.' Charlie gave the strange girl his warmest smile, and then shading his eyes with his hand, he looked into the sky and said, 'What was that?'

A tiny golden sphere flashed in the sunlight, and then vanished.

'That was the coach that brought us,' said Henry. 'It belongs to the forest.'

'A HEART-WARMING STORY FULL OF WONDER AND MAGIC'

JULIA ECCLESHARE, LOVEREADING

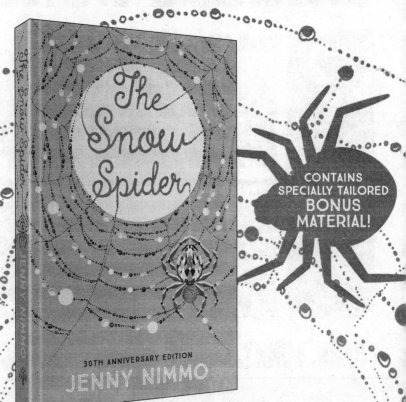

CONTAINS SPECIALLY TAILORED BONUS MATERIAL!

The Snow Spider

30TH ANNIVERSARY EDITION

JENNY NIMMO

'Time to find out if you are a magician, Gwyn'

Gwyn's grandmother leaves him five gifts: a brooch, a piece of dried seaweed, a tin whistle, a scarf, and a broken toy horse. She tells him they will help make him a magician – but can Gwyn use them to bring his missing sister, Bethan, home?